CHOOSE TO KILL

EMMY ELLIS

CHAPTER ONE

They were getting on his nerves. That was unexpected. He'd thought he'd be mesmerised by them, his whole being engrossed in every tiny thing they did, him in awe that he'd accomplished bringing the first of the little birds into his haven at last. But... No. He hadn't anticipated the complaints. And who were they to grumble about what he had in mind for them? How could they be so ungrateful?

Things hadn't quite gone right—and he'd been so meticulous, too. Fate had a nasty way of interrupting the flow, of putting her own ideas into the mix, and fucking with his plans like this had momentarily put him off-kilter. Why hadn't he covered every eventuality? He'd thought he had, yet here he was, annoyed, agitated at himself—and them.

Still, there was work to be done, even if they didn't behave in the way he wanted them to—work he'd looked forward to for a long time now.

One of them squirmed in the corner—the blonde, all thin legs and large bust spilling out of a top that would be right at home on a prostitute. He studied her from the bedroom doorway of the derelict house he'd brought them to, a place no one would think to come, what with it being boarded up, ready to be demolished. It had an eerie air, and only the faint sounds of rushing traffic from the main road on the outskirts filtered in.

The blonde huddled with her side against the wall, legs drawn up, resting her chin on her knees. And she *hugged* those knees—a lifeline, he reckoned—and stared at him through long strands of hair that streaked across her face, and they reminded him of insubstantial, spreading fingers. Her eyes glittered in the shaft of light coming through the open doorway, and her features

2

appeared pinched, as though she was unwell or under great stress.

He didn't understand that. The stress. The whining. Hadn't she listened to what he'd told her? That she was going to a better place and he would help her to get there? He'd wanted to call her ungracious when she'd told him he was a *shitfacemotherfuckingfreak*. Wanted to explain how she'd got it all wrong, that this life wasn't where she was destined to be. That he was doing her a favour by releasing her early so she could go to God and kneel at His feet. Experience the wonder of a place so different from this...this messed-up ball of a planet.

She hadn't understood *that* either. Had babbled about wanting to go home, hadn't she. The tears on her cheeks had almost glistened, the whites of her eyes a mesh of red spider veins that stretched from her blue irises, their tapering ends hidden beneath her upper and lower lids. Her lashes, clumped together from being damp, got him thinking of the ferns in his garden after a downpour, and he'd had a quick glimpse of that garden, his mind wandering to the tasks he had to perform there. Weeds had intruded while he'd been finalising his plans, and that wasn't to be tolerated. An untidy house and garden meant an untidy mind.

"Stop staring." He pushed off the doorframe and took a step back onto the landing. Glanced at what he'd brought with him, which leant on the wall beside the door. "And close your mouth. Looks like

3

you're catching flies." He wanted to laugh at that. Who caught flies with their mouth?

No one.

"Please, take me back home," she said, gaze fixed on him. A spiteful gaze.

Why would he want to take her home when she stared at him that way?

"No. Not yet. You're staying here for the time being."

He lifted the wallpaper-pasting table he'd bought from the hardware shop and walked into the room. She widened her eyes. Did she think he was going to lay her out on it, operate on her like some feral surgeon? The imagination was a strange yet wonderful thing. If only he could crawl inside her and see what was there. Maybe he'd taste her fear, sharp and acidic, or have the throb of her undulating pulse pounding through him in tandem with his. Maybe he'd sense her spite, although he sensed it now well enough.

Why had it turned out like this?

Why wasn't she smiling, eager to join Him?

And why wasn't she still asleep like the other one?

She ought to be thanking him. This world was no place for a little bird, no place at all. It held violence and mayhem, despicable people doing despicable things. The next few hours of his life were a means to an end, something he had to do in order to obey His command.

"Stand up, girl." He unfolded the table and set it up. Once done, he went out to the landing again to lift a wooden box. He carried it into the room and put it on top of the pasting table.

"What's in there?" she asked, ignoring his order.

Her voice had been full of fear, and he studied her for a moment—the wide eyes, her mouth clamped tightly shut, lips trembling—and tried to puzzle her out. Who wanted to cry at the thought of meeting Him? It just didn't make sense.

"Stand up, come over here, and you'll see." He unlatched the silver clasps on the front of the box and raised the lid. Put one hand inside and stroked the contents. Smiled at what they signified.

She stood then, remaining in the corner to watch him, possibly to judge whether it was safe to do as he'd asked. Of course it was safe. Everything about this scenario was—he'd ensured that much. Her journey was only partly travelled. She had a way to go yet, but the end of her road was in sight.

He paid her no mind, going outside the room to collect a sign he'd made. THIS WAY TO REST AT HIS FEET. He'd fashioned it from a rectangle of plywood and cut two corners off so it resembled an arrow, then attached it to a lengthy piece of four-by-four. He'd taken great pains to get the wording just right, the black, oil-based paint frequently dirtying his fingers, but it looked professional enough, as though it could stand proudly at any roadside, showing voyagers the route.

He walked towards her, the post of the sign in one hand, purposely left un-sanded so it seemed authentic, weathered. She pressed herself right into the corner, and he had no doubt she would have splayed her hands against the wall if she could. Her wrists being bound by rope and hanging in front of her put paid to that. Her ankles were tied, too. He hadn't wanted to bind her, but she'd been feisty, and that had been the only way to control her flailing arms and kicking legs.

He dismissed her after a concise glimpse, then resumed his task.

Before he'd found the little birds, he'd come here to prepare, screwing an iron post holder into the flooring. Now, he slotted the post into it and secured it in place with metal snaps. Those were a necessity and something he was glad he'd thought of, especially given her spirit. Otherwise, she might grab the post out and strike him with it.

He made sure the arrow pointed to the pasting table and stood back to admire his handiwork.

A fine sign. A beautiful sign.

"Come along." He returned to the box. "Don't you want to see what I have in here?"

She shook her head, and he frowned. Hadn't she just asked what was in the box? Why would she now decide she didn't want to inspect it? What had changed?

"What are you thinking?" He rested a hand on the contents, drawing circles with his fingertip over one item.

"That you're going to hurt me, you sick fuck! That you have knives or saws or a gun in there, and you're going to...*to fucking hurt me!*"

6

Oh, that didn't look pleasant, her face all screwed up like that. He frowned harder, wondering how he could make her pretty again, as she'd been when he'd called at her house before bringing her here.

"I'm not going to hurt you...yet." He smiled. "It's your choice as to how you make your journey. Your luck that will determine how you go. I will have to hurt you, yes, but it won't be my choice. Do you understand?"

It was obvious she didn't. Obvious she hadn't listened to him properly on the way over here. She'd been in the back of his car, slightly dopey from the drugs he'd slipped into her wine at her house. He'd gone to painstaking lengths to explain the wonderment that was Heaven, the kingdom where she'd be welcomed into His open arms. She'd squealed behind the balled material in her mouth—an extra-large handkerchief with the figure of Jesus embroidered in one corner—eyes bulging, her writhing as though she was having a fit.

She didn't want to be taken, didn't want to be on this journey, but she had no other option.

"Are you *sure* there's nothing harmful in there?" she whispered, looking at him with very different eyes now, the edges softened, the creases around them significantly shallower.

If he didn't know better, he'd say she was playing a game, veering onto a different track in order to make him think she was coming around to his way of thinking.

But he *did* know better.

"Nothing harmful at all." He smiled again.

She hopped once. Paused to balance herself. Continued across the room, feet thudding loudly. He would have glanced at the other little bird to see if the noise was waking her, but he didn't trust the blonde. He'd keep his wits about him until her journey was over.

She reached his side and kept her sights on his face, questions in her eyes she was probably dying to ask. If she wanted answers, she'd have to voice the queries—he wasn't about to help her out. One didn't get anywhere in this life by allowing others to hold the reins. You had to take a firm grip of them yourself and steer the horses, keep them in line and on course, otherwise your carriage was likely to topple and fall.

Slowly, she moved her gaze from him and peered inside the box. He followed suit, keeping her in his peripheral, on guard in case she thought she could lull him into a false sense of security and do him some damage. He stared at what she saw. His roulette wheel encased in a white surround, a Bible verse on the underside of the lid in fancy script. Ball bearings nestled in a slimmer box down the side, red dice at the bottom. What on earth was harmful about them?

She frowned hard, then turned to him. "What... What's that for?"

"That's your choice, that's what it is. The thing that will tell me what I have to do next. Your options."

"Options?" She gave the box her attention. Lifted her bound hands as though she were about to touch the wheel, then lowered them, perhaps realising, sensibly, that she really shouldn't put her mitts on it until he gave her permission.

"Yes, your choice. One spin of the wheel, and we'll know what course of action will help you on your travels to meet Him."

She jumped back one hop, and her gaze went to the door.

"You wouldn't get far," he said. "Probably fall down the stairs and hurt yourself. And then where would you be, hmm?" He nodded. "Yes, you'd be at the bottom, broken and bleeding, and even though that might be the way you choose to go when you spin the wheel—bleeding—the manner in which you were bleeding and broken isn't what He wants."

"Who is He?" She stared through the doorway.

He wondered if the light beckoned her. Whether the pull of freedom was so strong she fancied her chances of escape.

"My god. I told you that already." He gritted his teeth.

"I see."

"No, you don't."

"No..." She sighed, the sound of it more like a sob, and flicked her watery eyes to him. "No, I don't think I do."

He held up one hand, pointing towards the ceiling. "Ah, but all will soon be revealed. Spin the wheel." He nodded at the box, more of a sideways jerk of the head, and folded his forearms across his chest. "Go on, spin it."

She shuffled closer, rasping her feet on the floor. That noise, he didn't like it, and he held back a bark of irritation. Raising her hands, she placed them in the box and spun the wheel.

He stared at it, at the blur as the black and red segments bled into one another. "There, that wasn't so bad, was it? Now, that was just a practice. Next time, you'll throw a ball bearing— gently—onto the wheel as it's spinning, and we'll see where it lands once the wheel stops."

She stared at him, clearly uncomprehending. "And?"

He sighed. "I told you this in the car."

"I know, but I'd like you to tell me again. Please?"

Stalling. She was stalling for time.

"The colour it lands on will determine what happens."

"And that is?"

He inhaled deeply through his nose then let it out via his mouth. "If it lands on black you will enter the kingdom bruised."

"And red?"

"You will enter the kingdom...bloodied."

She moved as though to faint, and he reached out to catch her before she fell. If she was playing a game, she was a good actress. Her face paled, and her eyes rolled.

"Behave yourself!" He cradled her back in one arm while fanning her face with his free hand.

10

"This is not the correct form of conduct for one about to visit Him."

"Oh, dear God..." she whispered.

At last! She's getting it. He is a dear god.

"Indeed," he said. "Now, stand upright and act in a proper manner for one about to commence her journey."

She obeyed, although she swayed a little, and selected a ball bearing, held it in a tight fist. He contemplated whether she'd throw it at him, or use that fist to strike him, but she remained in place, appearing placid and all-serving, as he'd hoped she'd be.

"Spin the wheel." He nodded at her, eager to get this phase underway.

She did, then tossed the ball bearing into the box as though it had grown hot and had burnt her skin. As though it held her fate in its core. She stared at the wheel, as did he, and together they waited for it to slow, for the little silver orb to find a home on black or red. While waiting and keeping one eye on her, the other on the wheel, he pondered on what implements he would get to use. The sharp, shiny ones or the dull, heavy ones? No matter. Either way, he looked forward to holding them, to sending her off. After that, he'd perhaps take a breather then return to deal with the other woman.

And after *that?*

He'd start all over again, beginning with the selection process.

CHAPTER TWO

Detective Langham had arrived at the late-night scene around nine o'clock, tired as hell. He'd rushed out after only having been off duty a short time since the capture of David Courtier, the man responsible for the abduction and murder of several women. He'd worked damn hard on that case, forgoing his weekend off, and now, here he was on a Sunday evening, before he'd even had the chance to bring that recent case to a proper close, standing in the living room of a dead woman who had clearly been battered to death.

Jesus, will this shit ever stop?

Detective Fairbrother would usually have dealt with this, but he was no doubt standing in front of another similar scene himself. A report had come in that two women had been found like this. Langham had had no choice but to assess this scene while Fairbrother did the other.

Shortly, SOCO would eventually turn up, and Langham could make sure they were in place doing their thing. Once the ME, Hank, had arrived to give an on-scene report of how he thought the woman had died—obvious from what Langham could see—Langham would try to get hold of another senior officer to take over here. Then he could fuck off home.

The woman could have been any age—her features weren't exactly giving him a good indication. Her face had bloated from a beating, bruises deep maroon where blood had rushed to the surface of her skin. It never failed to stump him why people did something like this. All the books in the world on the subject could never fully explain it adequately. Yeah, he understood that most individuals who killed intentionally—more than once—had a 'calling', some inner voice or reason that 'made' them do it, maybe they'd even had a fucked-up childhood, but it didn't excuse their behaviour, did it? Didn't make it right.

Christ. Poor bitch.

From her clothing, he determined she was young—in her twenties or thirties, perhaps. Dark skinny jeans clung to her slim legs, and a halter-neck top, red with black zigzags, covered what he assumed would be a multitude of colours beneath, ranging from blue to that nasty maroon to black. Her arms and neck bore patches of bruising, lines of small ovals, probably from fingers, and larger, round-edged rectangles, possibly from fists.

She'd pissed someone off good and proper.

The alternative didn't bear thinking about, but he'd be thinking about it a lot over the coming days that someone had done this for fun. Before arriving here, Langham had hoped the two women being found like this was just a coincidence, that their other halves had lost the plot during an argument and had let fly with their fists, going a bit too far. It wasn't unheard of. A city this size was bound to throw up two, three, maybe more of the same incident on any given day or night. Domestics were common.

Except he'd been kidding himself. Upon his arrival, he'd taken a call on his mobile from Fairbrother, who'd asked him to check this woman for foreign objects. Turned out they both had ball bearings placed in their navels. Nothing coincidental about that.

Langham hated the fact that she'd been posed in a star shape on the laminate flooring, centre of the room, her killer having taken the time to position her. The man had been in no rush then—Langham assumed it was a man anyway. Whoever had done this hadn't felt threatened. He'd also brushed her blonde hair in a fan around her head. Her strappy, black high-heeled sandals told him she'd either been out to a pub or club, or had been intending to go when her killer had struck. If one man had murdered both women, he may well have known them—they weren't just chance pickings, which meant the victims possibly knew each other as well. Officers back at the station were doing background checks now and would find any useful information about that.

PC Hastings came to mind then. He was due back on shift in the morning, a young, green policeman on Langham's team who really ought not to be on it. He wasn't experienced enough, and the last murder case had been his first foray into realising the depraved depths some people's minds went to. Langham had told him he'd seen nothing yet with regards to the sick-to-look-at mess a victim could be, and come the morning, the lad would see Langham had been right.

Poor kid'll chuck his guts up when he sees the pictures of this woman.

SOCO arrived, pulling Langham out of his thoughts. They gathered in the hallway, white suits, a crowd of milk bottles. He beckoned them in.

"I haven't touched, just stood here and observed," he said.

16

One tech nodded, and they all got to work, the majority spreading themselves out in the room, the hallway, and a couple going upstairs. Three went into the kitchen just off the lounge, chattering about the new Aldi that had opened down Boswell Road.

Got to chat shit to keep sane.

Langham moved to the window, peering out to see which of the surrounding and opposite houses needed visiting first, to find out if anything had been clocked. The women's deaths had been reported to the station via anonymous phone calls, the voices disguised with one of those gadgets had them sounding metallic. Someone knew what they were doing and exactly how to do it. The dispatch centre had logged two mobile numbers, neither used before or since—clearly pay-as-you-go cheapies. Damn things were probably in a random bin by now, clear of fingerprints—*gloves, he'd have worn gloves*—buried beneath discarded rubbish.

He drew a quick sketch of boxes so that when he went out to the other side of the street, he could put house numbers inside them with stars next to those who he thought might have seen something. Made it easier for whoever took over here to know who needed an immediate visit and who could wait.

The houses sat directly in front of the pavements, meaning that if the killer had parked at the kerb at this house he could have knocked, got in, killed, and been gone, all potentially without anyone taking any notice. Curtains would have been drawn to shut out the bleak night, and he imagined no one at all would have seen a car draw up. Heard it maybe, but seen it? Chance would be a fine thing. Unless she'd been killed much earlier in the day. If so, why the sandals, the clubbing outfit? Had she been dead even longer? *She doesn't smell bad enough.* Was her outfit from Friday night and she'd been kept alive for a while?

If that were the case, the job would be harder. People—if they had seen something—tended to get details muddied after twenty-four hours had passed. He just had to hope this street had the usual nosy bastard in it, someone who always jumped up at the sound of a vehicle or loud footsteps, curtain twitching as they satisfied their curiosity as to who was outside. Someone who always remembered everything, even perhaps wrote it down.

The ME's car drove past. It came to a stop a few houses down, Hank on duty and not the other surly sods who tended to the dead. Hank had always reminded Langham of a ball on legs, his torso perfectly round, chubby arms jutting out either side. The man in question strutted along the pavement and squinted at the houses, then raised one finger as he obviously realised which house held the victim. He walked inside. Two SOCOs took long metal poles and white tarpaulin out from a van opposite.

The tent that would shield the lower front of the house from prying eyes.

Hank bustled in and stood beside Langham, glancing over his shoulder at the victim, *tsking*, then staring out of the window.

"Had a rush of them tonight, apparently," Hank said.

"What, victims like this one?" Langham frowned. He'd brain Fairbrother if he'd failed to pass on new information.

"No! Deaths, you silly bugger. That's why I'm here. Got called in for overtime. Need to pick up the other bird later as well. So, are you ready for me to take a quick gander?"

Langham swivelled to look at the victim. Two SOCOs worked around her, tweezers in one hand, evidence envelopes in the other. A third took photographs.

"No, not until they've finished." He faced the window again.

"Bloody hell." Hank put his hands on his hips. "Could have stayed at home for another couple of hours and finished watching *Pride and Prejudice*."

Langham chuckled. "What, *you* watching that?"

"Too bleedin' right. Keira Knightley does it for me every time."

They lapsed into silence. The men outside erected the pole system ready to drape the tarpaulin cover on top. The rustle of the protective suits behind him seemed ominous, creepy alongside the ticking of a wall clock and Hank's heavy breathing. Langham ought to be used to these noises, but he wasn't. He'd joined the force to do good, and, like PC Hastings, hadn't thought well enough to imagine he'd one day be the copper called out to scenes like this. He'd looked forward to wrapping the last case up, getting the paperwork done and filed, and forgetting that case until the trial. Being thrown so quickly into another with no respite… Well, he'd just have to deal with it, because no other fucker apart from Fairbrother or a lower ranked detective was going to.

He sighed. The men outside were nearly done with the poles. Just a few nuts to be tightened, and the houses opposite would vanish behind material. He glanced at Hank, who'd chosen that moment to stare at him.

"Do you ever wonder," Langham said, "whether there'll always be psychos? I mean, the nutjobs seem to have grown in number over the years. I don't remember hearing about them much as a kid."

Hank shrugged. "Maybe we were lucky. Shielded from the news and whatever. If you think about it, though, to the public, serials still seem few and far between. It's not often they hit the news. Look at ones in the past. We managed to keep some quiet. Reckon this one'll be the same. It's only the people who kill multiples that get in the public eye these days. One or two women…sounds nasty, but they can be swept under the carpet. But loads? No, it gets out. Only takes one copper to slip the word, and your job's made a damn sight harder."

Langham nodded. "Yeah, we see what's really going on, and if you think about it, if the public knew, there'd be mass panic."

"Exactly. If they knew how many bodies I tend to in my working day..." Hank ran a flattened hand down his face.

"We've just got to hope we can keep this one quiet then. Not a serial at the moment. Just the two of them. Like you said, swept under the carpet." Langham shook his head. "Shouldn't be that way, though. We shouldn't look at them as just a case to solve. They're people, for fuck's sake."

"Or they were." Hank cleared his throat. "From my side of the fence, when I'm working on them, I imagine what they did, who they were. What their favourite snack was or whether they had a hobby. I see them on the slab and think: What a waste, what an utter waste."

Langham nodded, turning to view the woman on the floor, then he took in the room. She'd liked to read, watch DVDs, going by the neat stacks on a large bookshelf against the back wall. A romantic. *Love Actually. Four Weddings and a Funeral.*

A creeping light change encompassed the room, dousing the brightness somewhat. He swivelled to face the window again, the tarpaulin now in place. It seemed nothing more than a marquee, something from an outside wedding reception. It brought to mind one of the DVDs and the fact that the woman may well have been to four weddings in her lifetime but hadn't bargained on her funeral being so soon.

21

"This is bullshit," he muttered.

"It is that." Hank sniffed. "There are times I get tired of this. Times when I wish I'd chosen another career. But then I think of what I'm doing, getting as much information from them as I can before I tidy them up and make them presentable. I tell myself I'm giving them their dignity back, giving their families a last viewing that might get rid of the images they've got in their minds of what their loved one ended up like after some killer's had a go at them. But with her?" He jerked his head to indicate the poor soul behind them. "The funeral home's got their work cut out for them. I don't think even they can make her pretty again."

CHAPTER THREE

Oliver rolled over onto his side in bed, disoriented, his throat dry. He swirled his tongue around, the thickness of it giving the impression that his mouth was full of material. He kept his eyes closed—could focus better that way—and waited for more information from the dead to filter through. Cold swept over his top half, goosebumps spreading out on his skin. He concentrated. Had the sensation of wearing a halter-neck top. He pushed for a colour. His skin burned in the places the top would have touched had he really been wearing it. Red, the top was red. That or dark orange. And black.

Something spun beneath his eyelids, red amongst black, so dark it gave him the shivers. He couldn't work out what it was, and no other indication was forthcoming so he could determine what he was seeing. Frustrated, he groaned, reaching out with his mind and silently asking for more, that whoever needed help had to clue him in better.

He stared at the whizzing red-and-black movement ahead.

A fist broke through the blur, connecting with his nose. It hadn't literally hit him, but it might as well have. His head felt as though it snapped back, yet it hadn't moved at all, and pain bloomed throughout his face, evil and with such intensity that he thought he might be sick. Another fist came, quick and without mercy, smacking his cheekbone, which cracked under the assault. God, whoever was contacting him had been through hell, and more was to come, he was sure of it. Hits rained on him, one after the other, seemingly without a break, and he took them all.

He pulled his *self* away from his body, letting the images and punches continue, absorbing the information surrounding the victim instead of

24

focusing on what was being done to him. A room without much in it except a pasting table with a box on top and a square pole of wood beside it jutting out of the floor. As the battering continued, he surged forward to look at that wood, frowning at the sight of an arrow-shaped plank attached to the top. There were words on it, black words, but he couldn't read them. Too fuzzy.

Oliver frowned. The items didn't make any sense, and rather than try to force the link between him and the spirit to emerge, he diverted his attention to behind the victim. A tooth jolted loose and trickled to the back of his throat. He swallowed, gargling on blood, and pushed the beating aside. He might not have long to process this information, and the more he could get, the better he could help the police.

A woman crouched in the corner, watching the victim being assaulted, her eyes wide, yet she appeared aloof, somewhat out of it. Oliver floated towards her, wanting to enter her body, yet knowing if he did, he might lose his strong connection with the victim. Instead, he pressed a small part of himself into the second woman's mind, leaving the majority tethered to the one in the red halter-neck.

The corner woman was next to be beaten, he sensed that keenly. She was being treated to a show, being given fair warning of what she was going to get. Far from feeling afraid, she was perplexed, thinking that what she was seeing was some drug-induced hallucination, a film she couldn't recall agreeing to watch. Oliver felt it all, both women's emotions, and battled to remain remote, to detach himself from the horror, the all-consuming grip they had on him.

Another tooth broke loose, again going down his throat, and punches found his gut, his back, his sides. He sensed the victim going down, a freefall that seemed to take forever before she hit the floor. And that floor was dusty, gritty, tiny hard particles digging into the tops of her arms. The woman in the corner widened her eyes, choked back a sob, and attempted to stand.

"Stay where you are," a man said, his voice full of gleeful malice.

One harsh kick to the victim's kidney had Oliver curling into a ball on his side. He retreated from the woman in the corner and hovered at the ceiling, the kicks coming in his peripheral, but he looked elsewhere, scouring the room in order to see the abuser. The trouble was, the victim had her eyes closed, was consumed by pain, and any visual of the man doing this to her wasn't in her head—or she wasn't willing to show him to Oliver.

Come on. Give me a glimpse of him.

He appeared then, as though materialising out of the darkness, a looming figure who seemed bigger than he actually was. The victim's fear had magnified him, yet he was slight, the kind of bloke you wouldn't glance twice at on the street. Unassuming, nothing to take any notice of, and wasn't that always the way? Killers were rarely big, hulking brutes, muscles on top of muscles and even more muscles on top for good measure. No, in Oliver's experience, they were what might be deemed as 'normal' everyday people, except their eyes... Yes, their eyes gave them away, with their evil glints or their blank, empty stares. In this case, the eyes were alive with excitement, sparkling almost, something that indicated he'd do this again—and very soon. He had the lust for bloodshed careening through his veins.

Quickly, Oliver branded his features into his memory: Shoulder-length brown hair, cowlick front right. Brown eyes. Wide mouth. Thin, pale lips. Prominent cheekbones, high mountains beneath sunken eye sockets. A slender nose, a deviated septum, the ball of flesh growing out of one side, almost filling his nostril. Handlebar moustache, brown with greying ends. Seventies rocker sideburns, out of place in this day and age.

No way would Oliver forget him now.

The man stepped back, glaring at Oliver, when in reality, when this had played out for real, he'd probably been staring at the woman in the corner. It was a creepy feeling to think he could see Oliver, that he knew he was there.

The abuser drew his foot back then swung it forward, the toe of his boot greeting the victim's nose. Pain speared Oliver's brain—bone had penetrated grey matter. Everything went black, although Oliver was still in that room, still in the presence of the killer, a dead woman, and another who'd be just as dead within a matter of minutes. He waited for more information, but all he received was a deathly calm, thick and cloying, wrapping itself around him and squeezing tight. He longed to withdraw, to get back into himself, where he was safe in bed. The reality of what he'd seen gripped him, and he rose, coming out of the vision, fighting off the urge to vomit. He was dumped with frightening speed back into his body.

Then he slept.

CHAPTER FOUR

L angham woke to the blare of his alarm clock,
some new-fangled pop song that grated on his
nerves. He blindly reached for his bedside cabinet,
jamming his finger onto the snooze button,
intending to use the extra nine minutes to become
fully awake. The time passed with him dozing. A

different song startled him from sleep, and he switched the music off properly then dragged his tired arse out of bed. He'd managed only a few hours and had one hell of a day ahead of him.

In the shower, as was usual, his current case was on his mind. He hadn't thought clearly last night, but there had been no signs of a struggle in the victims' homes. He'd bet his last quid they hadn't been beaten there. With any luck, the forensic report would be on his desk by the time he made it into work—that was a joke, but wishful thinking was a good quality to have when you had nothing else—and he'd gain some insight into where they may have been killed.

He dressed then went into the kitchen, leaning against the worktop while he waited for the kettle to boil. The rumble of it went some way to easing his frazzled nerves that were already pinging.

The doorbell rang, and he answered it. "You've got something?"

Oliver came in, shuffling to the kitchen. "Had a weird experience. That case you were called out on last night... Did it have anything to do with a woman wearing a red-and-black halter-neck?"

Langham's heart rate escalated. Jesus fuck, if Oliver had seen what Langham thought he'd seen...

"Yes." *Don't push him.*

"And she was beaten to death?"

"Yes."

"Another woman was, too. It was an empty room, with a box on a pasting table, and this signpost, but I couldn't read what it said. Grit on the floor. She... It was awful. They didn't go quickly. Just bloody awful..."

Langham couldn't resist asking, "Did you see the killer?"

Oliver nodded. "Male, about thirty-five to forty. Brown hair and eyes. Old-fashioned moustache and sideburns. I'll need to get hold of Sue the artist this morning so she can draw him. It was like he saw me, knew I was there. I can't get his face out of my head. And he's going to do it again. He *loved* what he was doing."

"Christ, don't they all."

The kettle boiled, the switch flicking off with a loud snap. Langham ignored it.

"I'll need to see the dead women first, before I do the picture." Oliver lifted his head to look at him. His eyes were watery, set back in sockets that were far too sunken. Grey beneath, the tops of his cheekbones too prominent.

Langham couldn't imagine what it was like for him, living his life constantly touched by whispers from the dead unless he channelled them out. "I'll take you."

"Thanks." Oliver sniffed.

The morgue was a bastard for giving Langham the chills. Yeah, it was cold for a reason, but those other chills... Shit, he doubted he'd ever feel comfortable down there. Hank was doing overtime. The poor sod appeared as though he'd

31

been slapped hard and was still taking a beating. Langham winced at his turn of thought. Not particularly a good thing to think, considering those women were in two fridge drawers, their spirits undoubtedly wishing they weren't. What decisions had they made prior to their deaths that had meant they'd either gone willingly with that killer or had been in the wrong place at the wrong time so he could abduct them?

Hank had been working on an elderly woman as Langham and Oliver had entered, and, after a gentle stroke to the dead lady's hair and the reassurance that he wouldn't leave her alone for long, he'd led them from the exam room and into another, his rubber-soled shoes squeaking as he made his way over to the fridges.

"Oliver," he said, resting his fingers on his forearm, "these two... Well, they're not pretty, all right?"

"I know." He eyed the bank of metal doors that shielded people who'd had their lives either snatched away too soon or those who had longed for death at the end of a hopefully wonderful and fulfilling journey. "I've already seen the state of one of them. The blonde." He closed his eyes for a second or two, taking a deep breath.

Hank nodded. "Saw it, did you?" He opened one of the drawers until half the victim's shrouded body was visible. "This is Tina. If you need a natter with Lisa, she's in number sixteen." He glanced up at Langham. "I'll leave you to it."

Langham waited for Hank to go, then peeled back the sheet covering Tina Mason, who'd been twenty-two but seemed no age at all now. The bruising on her face appeared worse than it had during the night.

Oliver reached out and placed his gloved hand on Tina's forehead, his shoulders rising with his long intake of breath. He exhaled. "Jesus, the information with this one is coming on strong. He drugged them, but Hank will know what with. He took them from their houses. They were meant to be going on dates with him—had met him in a club a few weeks ago—so he'd built up their trust."

Langham refrained from swearing.

"Tina got into his car, and once she'd put her seat belt on, he clicked the locks then jabbed her in the thigh with a needle. It took seconds for the drug to work. She was with it but not, knew what was happening but couldn't do anything about it. Couldn't move. He drove out of her street and to a country road—seems like the one on the way to Harsden to me—then stopped to stuff a handkerchief in her mouth. It had an embroidered Jesus in one corner, she remembers that clearly. Then he bundled her into the back seat, and that's when she realised they weren't alone. Lisa was there, too, out for the count, slumped against a rear door."

The last case had a needle involved. What the hell?

Oliver inhaled deeply again, let the air out, then continued. "He went on about Him, as in God, and said that He had told him to do this."

Langham shook his head. Why did so many of them use God as their justification? Did they really believe a higher power was telling them how to behave, or was it just a cop-out excuse to make them feel vindicated in what they were doing? He'd never understand them, never.

"Oh God," Oliver whispered.

"What is it?" Langham's stomach muscles tightened.

"I left too soon last night. When I was having the vision, I mean. I would have found out more if I'd stayed to watch Lisa's death. I need to see her." He took his hand from Tina's brow then covered her face with the sheet. Slowly pushing the slab back into the fridge, he stared at the mound surrounded by darkness inside. Closed the door. Sighed. "Lisa has something to say."

Langham moved along the doors and located the correct fridge. He pulled the door open, then dragged the slab out. Lifting the sheet, he didn't fully take her in. He couldn't. It hurt too damn much to think that these people had been so full of life once.

Oliver pressed his clean-gloved hand to Lisa's forehead and once again sucked in a breath. Langham stood behind him.

"He told her they're his weekend hobby," Oliver said. "That he's got enough women lined up that will last him well into the next six months."

"Lined up?" Langham asked. "Can you get anything more concrete on that?"

Oliver nodded several times, clearly listening to Lisa's voice or seeing images that he could patch together to form a story. "He met them all at Chains."

"What? Where's that?"

"Some...um... Think it's a sex place. Yes, he chatted them up and arranged dates, got to know them. Managed to get them to give him their phone numbers. He told Lisa he was annoyed he'd had to give two beatings in one night instead of a good old slice. That the women's choices had denied him the pleasure of blood."

Langham had to stop himself from repeating him. Good old slice? A stabbing? "Choices? What the hell does that mean?"

"I don't know."

Oliver had sounded defeated, upset that he hadn't been able to get more. Langham held his breath for a moment, staring at the ceiling and offering a silent prayer that they'd get a break on this before that madman had a chance to practise his hobby over the coming weekend.

"A roulette wheel." Oliver's shoulders tensed.

Langham wanted to ask what the fuck he was talking about but knew that the images Oliver saw didn't necessarily match anything to do with the cases. They could signify something else entirely.

"That's how they made their choices," Oliver said quietly. "He's sick. Very sick. They have to spin the wheel, and... And if it lands on black, he kicks and punches them to death..."

"And red is stabbing," Langham finished. Jesus Christ, what the hell were they dealing with here? He'd met some strange bastards in his time, but this form of choosing how to kill was a new one on him.

"The killer prayed for red," Oliver said. "And He didn't listen. The man's hoping that God will let him have two reds next time."

"God has nothing to do with this," Langham muttered. "Anything else?"

"No. Oh, yes..."

Langham waited, holding his breath again.

"The man said, just before he stomped on Lisa's face for the last time, that he'd be going to Chains tonight to watch a show."

"Right," Langham said.

"Will I go with you?" Oliver busied himself putting Lisa back in the fridge, then leant on the closed door with his eyes shut. "I can still see him in my head. I'll know him if he's there."

Langham sighed. "Yes, you'll be coming with me."

CHAPTER FIVE

He studied the women in Chains, dissatisfied with the selection on offer. Some of those on his list were there, but they were in the 'maybe' column. The kind who might kick up a fuss or who he felt might not be as compliant as he'd first thought. He was confident he could deal with them

37

if he had to, but why bother if someone more suitable was available?

He stared around—filthy bitches, the lot of them, flaunting themselves for all to see—and a twinge of annoyance tweaked his gut. This place... Full of deviants, people who liked pain and torture in the bedroom. Well, he was only giving his chosen ones what they wanted in the end.

After the last two had gone to meet Him, he'd returned home and weeded the garden, albeit in the early hours of the morning. There had been enough light that he'd seen those wily green demons sprouting from his usually pristine grass and flowerbeds, and within a couple of hours, a job he'd neglected had finally been completed.

He wouldn't allow such slackness to happen again.

He adopted a less rigid pose and strode around the main area casually. It appeared much like a nightclub, with music playing, multi-coloured lights streaking, and people loosening up, dancing or talking in huddles.

He sipped his Coke and gazed at a few other men. Some of them didn't look like they could control anyone, but then again, when he'd stared at himself in his get-up before he'd gone to collect Tina and Lisa, he hadn't appeared the type who could subdue anyone either. He held back a bark of laughter. The shock on their faces when he'd turned up on their doorsteps with his wig, fake moustache, and sideburns. He'd had to make out he was taking them to a fancy-dress party. Of course, they'd protested that they hadn't known, and if they had they'd have dressed up, too, but he'd assured them that going as a clubber would be quite adequate.

Just a shame they hadn't enjoyed the party as much as he had.

Yet it hadn't been as thrilling as he'd thought it would be. With two beatings in one night... He sighed, telling himself not to dwell on that. There would be those in the future who dropped the ball onto the spinning wheel, and their fate would come up red. He hadn't tried the knife. Had been tempted to with the second woman but he'd resisted.

He sniffed, the inside of his nose a little tight, sore, where he'd ripped the prosthetic skin from his septum and put it in his pocket. The idea of that little facial oddity had come to him in a dream, where a monster had had a similar feature. Small things like that tended to stand out to people, something they remembered more than anything else. Like a scar across a cheek or a severe cleft in a chin. If he'd been seen in his disguise, yes, they'd remember his weird nose all right.

He had the urge to get back into his new self as soon as possible. That wig and whatnot had changed him, given him the strength he'd needed to pull off what he'd done. It had been the first time he'd truly felt himself, hence him venturing out tonight to secure another woman who was ready for her final journey. The next weekend wasn't long in coming, so to have a young lady agree to join him for a night out would need to be secured tonight or tomorrow. If she backed out in between now and the weekend, it would give him time to pick another from his list.

He elbowed through the crowd towards a door at the rear. A beefy bouncer nodded at him and pushed the door open. The empty room on the other side reminded him of a performance hall. Tiers of red chairs like bloodied teeth stretched out in a semicircle before him, and he wondered if that was yet another good sign. Bloody teeth.

Aisles with steps led down to the main circular area below. At the back, a stage, complete with red velvet curtains, hid whatever lay beyond. He imagined some tart there, trussed up and ready to take a beating, kneeling and willing to accept whatever punishment was sent her way. A thrill pulsed through him, and he quickly went down the stairs then opted to sit in the front row where he could get a good view.

He wondered how long it would be before other people joined him. When he'd have to share his space with those perverts. A shudder of revulsion replaced the thrill, and mean thoughts swirled in his head. It had been the way of his life, people spoiling it. If he had happiness, it was guaranteed someone would come along and mess it up. Make him unhappy. His mother had once told him that it was down to him, that only *he* gave people the ability to upset his apple cart. He'd thought about that for a long time and had come to the conclusion that she'd been right, so he'd concentrated on screening his emotions. He hadn't quite mastered it, but he was getting there.

Sitting bolt upright, he threw the revulsion off and thought of nicer, better things. For him to practise his calling, he had to mingle with folk he normally wouldn't be seen dead with. And if that was what God wanted, that was what he would do. It wasn't just the women's journeys he was dealing with, but his own. God was possibly testing him, testing his devotion, and what was a little discomfort every now and then?

The squeak of the door opening had him turning to see which deviant was entering. It wasn't just one but several, a gaggle of young women he suspected were here for an evening of being shocked, possibly here just for fun. Something to write about on that Facebook place when the night had come to its end. *Fifty Shades* had spawned a new wave of sexual awareness.

One of the women on his list stared down at him from the top step with a smile so bright he knew he was well on the way to securing His next angel, another little bird.

She'd chosen a demure outfit. A slinky black dress, albeit shorter than he would have liked, the hem resting just above her knees. A fitted black leather jacket. Knee-high black boots—he couldn't see the heel height from where he was—over legs either covered by a fake tan or sheer stockings. Her bright-red hair stood out in stark contrast to her clothes. She was certainly striking.

Striking. Perhaps he would be doing that to her soon.

"Hey, you!" she called, raising one hand and waggling her slim fingers.

He returned the gesture and contemplated standing, offering for her to sit beside him, but decided against appearing so eager. If she was meant to be his next project, He would make it so.

With difficulty, he turned to face the stage, as though she meant nothing to him. He'd watched people and had noted that disinterest bred interest. If she thought he wasn't too enamoured with her, and she liked him enough, she'd be compelled to make him like her back.

He listened to the group clattering down the stairs, their giggles and whispered chatter getting on his nerves. His mother's advice came to him again, and he breathed in deeply, scrubbing away the annoyance the women's actions had set off in him.

Smile—that was another thing his mother had told him.

'If you smile, even when you don't want to, it makes you more contented, son.'

He tried it. Found it worked marginally, so smiled harder. Wider.

Mother was usually right.

He missed her.

The young girl in the black outfit plopped down beside him, rudely wrenching him from his thoughts. Again he smiled, but it was so hard to control those surges of infuriation—they came unbidden—and it took a moment to compose himself. He turned to look at her and waited for her to speak first.

"I'm so glad you're here," she said, her voice a breathless flutter. "I've been coming back and coming back, hoping I'd see you, and now, here you are."

"Yes, now here I am."

"What have you been up to?" She tilted her head.

He held back a chuckle. If he told her exactly what he'd been 'up to', she'd be out of her seat and away from him in an instant. "Nothing much. You?"

He didn't care for what she'd been doing—not the boring, mundane things she was sure to tell him about—but those little snippets that would inform him whether he needed to be careful? Those were vital.

"Me neither. To be honest"—she leant closer so the tops of their arms met—"I've been thinking about you." She blushed.

He didn't find it endearing like he probably should have.

'If you smile, even when you don't want to…'

"Really?" He feigned surprise. "Funny you should say that, because I've been thinking about you, too."

Though not you specifically, and not for the reasons I'll let you think.

"Oh my God." She lifted one hand to rest the tips of her fingers over her lips. "That's just so wonderful!"

He watched her friends in his peripheral. They sat maybe ten seats along and seemed to be discussing him, throwing furtive glances his way, their mouths working but no words reaching him.

Whispering. Girls always whispered when gossiping.

"Isn't it?" he said. "Maybe we're fated."

"D'you think?"

Oh, she would be easy.

"How about"—he eased even closer to her—"we meet up this weekend?"

"Really?"

"Really. We could go to a party I've been invited to. Fancy dress." He'd learnt from last time—better to prepare her.

She let out a peal of excited laughter.

He smiled. Hard.

"Oh, that would be so much fun." She flashed her teeth at him. "What are you going as?"

"No idea yet," he said, knowing he'd be wearing his special outfit, his new skin. Being his proper self. "You?"

"I don't know." She chewed her bottom lip and stared into space, probably imagining herself in various costumes. "There are so many things I could be."

He nodded. "How about an angel?"

"Hmm, I could do..."

"Because that's how I see you. An angel."

44

Her cheeks blazed redder. "Oh, you're so sweet. An angel it is then. Where will we meet?" She rested her head on his shoulder.

Too familiar. Too much. Get. Off. Me.

"I can pick you up if you like. If I remember rightly, you said you lived on the end of a terrace down Fitz Road. That's not too far from me."

She squealed.

He cringed.

"How come I've never seen you about if we live so close?" she asked.

He shook his head. "No idea, but you'll be getting to know me pretty well come the weekend if I have anything to do with it."

He grinned inwardly.

She was his.

CHAPTER SIX

Oliver stepped through the rear door of Chains and blinked several times. He'd never been in such a place before, and to see an auditorium-type room had been the last thing he'd expected. He'd thought the show would have been on the dance floor.

"All right?" Langham asked.

Oliver nodded.

"You'll see some things that look like they should be performed in a dirty alley by thugs," Langham said, leading the way down the stairs. "You know, people being beaten while they get their jollies."

"It's controlled, apparently. Rules are followed," Oliver said.

"So I've heard. Not my cup of tea."

They reached the bottom of the stairs, and Langham picked two empty seats in the front row.

After sitting, Oliver explained what he knew of this type of lifestyle. He'd looked it up on the internet before they'd set off. "This show, what people do... It isn't hitting, not in the way you'd think of it. It's what they want."

"Exactly," a man beside Langham said, shifting around so he faced them. "They *want* to be hit, and those who do the hitting *want* to strike. *Need* to strike." He smiled somewhat tightly. "Pardon me for interrupting. Rude of me."

"No, no, that's fine," Oliver said.

Langham didn't look at the man but continued to stare straight ahead, a tic flickering in his jaw. All right, they hadn't expected to come here, but all leads had to be followed.

The man stuck out his hand. "Joe Adams."

Oliver shook it. A tingle shot up his arm, and he recognised it as a sign that at some point this man would feature heavily in his life. He got that sensation sometimes and waited for more feelings

48

to emerge that would tell him whether his involvement with him would be good or bad. Nothing came, so he relaxed a little.

A young redheaded woman peered around Joe from the next seat and said, "I'm new to this."

"Oh, so this show will be your first, too?" Oliver asked, thinking it best to act like they were here for leisure and not work.

He channelled to pick something up from her. A sense of needing to escape swept through him, but he wasn't sure whether it was coming from Langham, who was sitting there so rigidly and would undoubtedly be counting down the minutes until they could leave, or whether the feelings were radiating from the redhead herself. There were too many people here for Oliver to concentrate properly, too many chattering.

The lights dimmed, and everyone hushed, preventing further conversation. A spotlight beamed from behind them, creating a yellow circle on the curtains. One of them wafted, as though moved by someone from behind. Classical music filtered in, quiet at first, growing in volume gradually. The curtains swept open, and Oliver held his breath, adrenaline spiking, streaming through him until he thought he might pitch forward from the force of it—someone else's feelings were coming through, into him. Exhilaration heavily doused with aggression. He opened his eyes and glanced around. The auditorium was packed. Who the hell was feeling this way?

The stage was occupied by a blond man, getting ready to accept whatever was going to happen.

I want to see how it's done, a man thought. *I want to get it right when I do it.*

Oliver held still, hoping for more. No alarm bells rang. No sense of which man the voice belonged to. Nothing at all except anticipation and the sense of wanting the show to get underway.

It could have been any bloke in this room, bar Langham.

Oliver sent out a message for help from the dead, for a spirit to guide him to the person he and Langham were seeking. The visual shrank to just the front row, and he glanced first left, then right, gauging how many seats there were and who filled them. There must be twenty each side of the aisle, and many were occupied by women. He couldn't see clearly enough, what with the subdued lighting, so estimated that maybe thirty men were on his watch list—a far greater amount than he'd had to cope with in the past. With a sharp intake of breath, he closed his eyes.

Come on. Come out and hit him. Kick him. Punch him, the man thought.

Oliver sat rigid, waiting for more.

Kick and punch him until he can't get up. Until he's aching to breathe. Until he can't breathe anymore.

Oliver darted his torso forward, eyes open, flicking his head side to side to catch an uncontrolled facial expression from the men on the front row. It was too dark, damn it, and he

50

couldn't get a grip on which direction the voice had come from. He sat back and closed his eyes again. He was here. The man they were looking for was here. Who else would say such a thing?

I want her to enjoy what I'm going to do. Not like the other two, complaining. Ungrateful, that's what they were. They'd been like spoilt children, not getting exactly what they'd wanted for Christmas. Well, next time will be different. I reckon I'll buy some steel-toed boots for this weekend.

Oliver's stomach muscles clenched to the point of bringing pain. His instincts screamed that he should get up and find this man before he did any more damage. Before he killed again and shattered not only his victim's life but those of the people who loved her. Someone was out there, with no idea that she would be next. Someone was out there who had met him here, thinking he just wanted to take her out on a date.

Someone who would die if Oliver didn't find him soon enough.

CHAPTER SEVEN

This was *not* how he'd thought things would go. Everyone around him appeared to be fornicating. Filthy perverts, all of them, grabbing at one another. The redhead reached across and stroked him. He slapped his hand down on hers and removed it, distraught that she wanted what

53

everyone else was doing. What the man on the stage was doing.

"Not here," he whispered. In order to snare her, he had to play the game, let her think he was as up for it as she was. "I prefer privacy."

"Okay," she said. "I didn't mean…"

"No, it's fine, honestly."

It was far from fine, but he could hardly tell her that.

He glanced down at his watch, pressing the button on the side to illuminate the face. "Good Lord, I have to get out of here. Are you still up for Friday night? To be my angel?"

Her eyes brightened. "Do you remember my house number?"

"Yes, of course. Fifty-seven."

"What time will you come?"

"Would eight suit you?" That would give him time to take her to the house and get her situated before he set her final journey in motion.

"That's great," she said.

He rose then turned for the stairs. He took them two at a time. A bouncer at the top cocked his head, a silent question as to whether he wanted to leave. He nodded that he did, exiting, blasted with a slap of loud music that had been silenced when he'd been in the auditorium. His ears assaulted, he tried to think, to get used to the sudden noise, and made his way to the bar. He needed a bloody drink.

After asking for a Coke, he glanced around while the barman filled his order. People were getting drunk, prancing around looking nothing more than imbeciles. Why didn't they realise alcohol deadened the senses rather than heightened them? He could have his pick of any woman here now. The state they were in, they'd never sense he was bad for them.

He paid for his Coke and leant against the bar, one arm on top of it. Relaxed a bit. Until the redhead streamed towards him, a frown in place that she quickly masked by smiling. She came up to him, pressing her body into his. He couldn't move away without appearing rude, but, Lord, he wanted to. He didn't like her touching him. Didn't like her close proximity.

"I thought you said you had to go," she said, her tone slightly accusing.

"I thought it was later than it was. Read my watch wrong. I needed a drink anyway, and it was getting a bit much for me in there." He jerked his head in the direction of the auditorium.

"Oh, I know what you mean. Wasn't that *insane*? Another show started after that one. The proper torture one."

What? "Really?" Damn, he'd left too soon, had lost out on getting tips for his missions. "Would you want someone to do that kind of thing to you—what we saw in the other room?"

"It's too violent. I don't like it."

It didn't matter whether she liked it on Friday or not—if her ball landed on black, she'd be getting a bashing anyway. A thought hit him. Maybe, if she didn't like the idea of being struck, he'd get the chance to slash. Perhaps God had chosen her purposely, knowing she didn't like being punched. She may well prefer the blade.

"What about knives?" he asked.

"As long as they don't cut me," she said.

Oh, they'll be cutting you...

He tried not to laugh. "I think I'm going to head off."

"Oh."

"Seeing as I live by you, would you like a lift?" He could handle that. Put his head down when outside and keep it low until they reached his car, which he'd parked in a dark side street.

"All right then." She smiled. "I'll text the girls, let them know I'm going."

Ah, that was a special piece of information. She told people where she was going, kept in touch. He'd have to remember that on Friday night.

That phone of hers. He'd have to get rid of it pretty quickly.

"Glad to see you're safety conscious," he said. "Wouldn't want anything bad to happen to my angel." Before she could gush over that, he took her elbow. "Come on, let's get you home in one piece."

How he didn't laugh at that he didn't know. Hopefully, the next time he took her home she'd be in bits.

He guided her through the club and outside. With his head bent, he put an arm around her shoulders, as he imagined she'd expect, and led her along the pavement. She was texting already, so he didn't have to speak to her. It gave him a moment to think about things. At the corner, he took a left into the dark side street, pleased the bulb in the lamppost beside his car had given up the ghost. No one in the houses, if they peered outside, would be able to get a good look at him.

He clicked his key fob and stared at her over the roof of his car. She was still texting. Rather rude, that. How long did it take to send one message?

"In you get," he said, managing not to sound testy.

They both got in at the same time, and the momentum of their movement had their shoulders bashing. He shuddered inwardly but grinned at her, wondering if he appeared sinister in the murkiness. She smiled back, seemingly at ease, and he started the car, waiting for some banal comment or other to spew out of her mouth. He reminded himself he only had this car journey to suffer through, and next time they were together he'd be issuing orders and explaining where she'd be going. He hoped she was a little brainier than the last two, who hadn't understood what he'd told them.

That still rankled.

She chattered away on the journey, musing on where she'd get a set of angel's wings. She could use a white sheet as her dress, she said, and she had a pretty pair of white sandals that would do the trick. But the halo, now, that would be difficult. She'd go to Toys R Us and see if there was one there.

The outfit doesn't matter. He gritted his teeth. *No one except me is going to see it. Not until after you're a real angel anyway.*

The image of blood against a white sheet filled his mind, and he had to swallow to get rid of the lump of excitement that balled in his throat. He felt giddy and almost went over the speed limit at one point, such was his enthusiasm. He remembered just in time that being pulled over for speeding wasn't something he could afford.

At last, he slotted his car between two others outside her house and left the engine running while she busied herself unlatching her seat belt. She seemed to take an interminable amount of time, and he had to smile brightly to combat the urge to punch her in the temple. Pleased that his mother's advice had yet again worked—he was calmer, more in control now—he prayed she wouldn't want to sit and chat.

"So," she said. "I'll see you at eight on Friday night then."

"You will indeed."

She leant across and pressed her lips to his cheek. They were warm, and she breathed on him, the air hot and not at all pleasant. She smelt of too much perfume, all flowers and spice, and it took a lot of concentration for him to block it out. Thankful that she sat back, he waited for her to open the car door and get out. She bent down, waving at him through the window.

He regretted parking here. He'd have to wait until she finally moved before he could nose the car away.

Waving back, he watched her walk between his car and the one in front. She waved yet again—*will you just fuck off inside?*—and blew him a kiss. He blew one back, feeling utterly ridiculous, then eased out of his spot, wanting to belt down the road to get away from her as quickly as possible.

It wasn't until he'd left her street that he relaxed. He couldn't understand how she'd believed him when he'd told her he lived by her.

Who would want to live there?

CHAPTER EIGHT

Oliver had had enough. The show was too much. He leant closer to Langham. "I need to go."

Langham nodded, and they walked out. Relieved to be in the fresh air, Oliver took a hearty breath.

"Are you all right?" Langham asked.

"I am now. I heard him in there, you know. The killer."

"What did he say?"

"He was there to see how a beating was done properly." Oliver stared at the star-littered sky. "But I couldn't figure out exactly where he was. Front row, I know that much. Those I managed to get a decent enough look at weren't anything like the man I saw killing those women."

"So we're back to square one. No matter."

It sounded like it did matter.

A whisper tugged at the back of Oliver's mind, and he went rigid, waiting for more. He strained to hear the words, but they were nothing more than the sound of leaves rippling in the wind.

"Someone's trying to get through," he said.

"Related to the case?"

"I don't know. They're whispering. Can't make out what... *Shh*. Hang on..."

"He's been here. Gone now. Down the street. Follow me."

Oliver snapped his eyes open and glanced left then right. Left pulled at him, and he led the way. Langham never said a word, just followed. On the corner, left tugged at Oliver again, and he walked down the street, pausing beneath an unlit streetlamp.

"The trail stops at this spot. He was parked here," he said.

He peered around. A light was on in someone's living room. The curtains were open, and the silhouette went past the window.

Langham turned to where Oliver was facing. "I'll go over there, see if they saw anyone."

They crossed the street, and Oliver trailed behind him through an open metal gateway and up a cracked, concrete path.

Langham knocked on the door. "Let's hope they don't mind being visited at this time of night." He smoothed his jacket lapels.

The door opened. A man stood there in joggers and a grey T-shirt, one side of his blond hair mussed where he'd probably been lounging on his sofa. "Yeah?"

He had every right to be annoyed at them visiting him, but Oliver got the swift sense that it was more than that. That one word he'd uttered— spat out—had been trimmed with him hiding something, that people knocking on his door after dark was more than just an inconvenience.

"DI Langham, and my associate, Mr Banks." Langham took his ID out from his inside jacket pocket and held it up.

The man hid his alarm well, keeping his face composed, but inside he was clearly bricking it. "Yeah?"

"Sorry to bother you at this time of night." Langham replaced his ID. "I wonder, did you happen to look out of your window this evening, within, say, the past half an hour?"

The man glanced down at his watch. "Yeah."

"Did you see anyone?"

He thought for a moment, and in his head, Oliver saw what he'd seen. The lamppost going out, him getting up to see what was going on. Him glancing up and down the street, spying a couple in the darkness walking down the road, the woman texting, her phone partially lighting them up.

"Yeah. Some couple. Got into a car. Over there where the light's busted."

"Anything unusual about them?" Langham asked.

"Nah, just a normal couple, innit."

Oliver stared at the images floating through his head, thankful the spirits had transferred them from the resident's mind to his. He zoomed in on the man and woman. Gasped. Brought a hand up to his throat.

Langham swivelled round. "Everything all right?" He narrowed his eyes.

"Yes." Oliver backed down the path. "Thank you for your time, sir," he said to the man.

Langham turned back to the house owner. "Yes, thank you. You've been very helpful."

Oliver bumped into the gatepost, the edge of it jabbing his hip. He made it out onto the pavement then crossed the road to stand in the space the car had occupied.

Langham joined him. "What did you get?"

Oliver stood still, thinking, reaching out. "It was the couple sitting next to you."

"What?" He raised his eyebrows.

"Yeah, and the car, I think it's a...I'm getting Ford, but I don't know what type. And because of the light being out... It's dark in colour, that's all I can give you."

"Jesus Christ..." Langham tunnelled his hand through his hair. "We were sitting by him all that time?"

Oliver shook his head. "It seems so, but it wasn't him. The man next to you wasn't the man the spirit showed me. His hair was short, for one, and he didn't have that weird lump inside his nose, or a moustache and those sideburns."

"So what then? He could have shaved the 'tache off, had his hair cut." Langham dropped his hand to his side.

"I don't know. I'm as confused as you are. Maybe he's associated with the killer and that's why I picked up on him. The feelings I got in the club... Excitement, interest, anticipation."

Langham nodded. "But at least we have something. I'll go back to the station, run a check on Fords, get someone to look at the CCTV footage. We might get lucky and see them leaving the club." He paused, then, "And the armrests. They might have prints on them." He sighed. "There's going to be one unhappy club owner and hundreds of pissed-off people this evening."

"You're going to have the club shut down?"

"Just for tonight, yes. That chair needs dusting for prints, and the staff and customers need questioning. I know he doesn't look like the right man, but any lead is better than nothing. For all we

65

know he might be an accomplice. The one who picks up the women."

Oliver shook his head, stomach knotting, a signal that Langham had got it wrong. "No. No, he picks them up himself, I'm sure of it. I don't know why they don't look the same, but the man we're after is the one who sat beside you tonight." He paused, inhaling deeply. Saw both men standing side by side. The long hair of one slid off his head, and his moustache lifted from his face on one side. "Disguise," he said, convinced of it. "The bastard wears a disguise."

At the station, Oliver made himself a coffee while Langham went about his business. Oliver sat at Langham's desk and debated whether to do some filing for him or just sit and think. To just sit and think won, so he leant back and closed his eyes. He thought about the evening, starting from the moment they'd walked into the club. Examining things from the outside in, watching himself as if he were someone else entirely, might throw up something he'd missed.

The front of the club hadn't given him much at all, just feelings of people being drunk and out for a good time. The auditorium was where he'd had a shift in his senses. He thought about what time he and Langham had gone in there. It might help to narrow things down on the CCTV footage—if the club even had any. Most of the seats had been filled, and they'd been lucky to find two empty on the front row.

He purposely ignored the stage and looked across at the man sitting beside Langham. He appeared so *normal* that it was beyond his comprehension as to how he could have killed those women. But a body was a brilliant disguise for a warped mind. What went on inside heads sometimes didn't match the outside. What the hell had driven him to want to kill? What had happened in his life that meant he had urges no sane person would have? Oliver didn't know, and it was pointless trying to work it out. His job was to help find him, and he had to be caught.

He shifted his attention to the redhead. The responsibility to find the killer weighed heavy on his mind. And why was that man even killing? Because he claimed God had told him to choose her? Because he was hiding behind the god thing to save himself any culpability? Oliver's take on it was that he just had it in him to kill—whether by choice or owing to the way he'd been brought up and how he'd been programmed to think, he didn't know—and no amount of pinning it on God would wash with the police or a jury. The man needed psychiatric help, yet he hadn't appeared mental at all. Rude to have butted into their conversation, yes, but not mad.

Those garbled whispers came again, as though too many spirits clamoured to get through. Oliver hated it when that happened. He imagined them all pushing at a chink in the veil that separated this world from theirs, and the gap just wasn't wide enough for them all to slip through. Faces materialised, one stacked on top of the other, indistinct and transparent, pressed to a four-inch-wide slit, as though there was literally a wall between the two realms. Lisa and Tina were there, eyes showing their fright, but their bruises had gone.

Tina opened her mouth, a gaping maw, a circle of blackness in an otherwise white face. Numbers spewed out of it, through the gap, and headed towards Oliver. He reached out and caught one, looked down at it resting on his palm. It was a red nine.

Red.

This time the killer was going to wield a knife. And he'd use it on Saturday, not Friday. Saturday was the ninth of the month.

They didn't have long to find him. He'd killed on a Friday before. What would happen to make that change? What events waited in store to thwart his previous pattern?

Oliver hoped they got to the redhead before she could find out.

CHAPTER NINE

At the station, Langham had put an officer to work on all the Fords in the area, another couple were studying the street CCTV, and he had sent two uniforms to the club with instructions that no one was to leave. A call had been made to SOCO, who would be en route, ready to scour the area where the man had sat. This would prove to be a big operation. The club had to have had thousands in it, and some of them might not be too pleased at being told they had to be questioned by the police. He suspected many would have been at the show in secret. The idea that their desires might be made public if they'd spotted the man and had to give evidence at trial wouldn't be something they'd want to have happen. Still, he had a job to do, and if anyone was reluctant to get involved and lied to save their own embarrassment, they could live with the next victim's blood on their hands.

Yes, he understood how something like this could throw up all manner of questions from loved ones, and that being accepted for what they enjoyed would be anathema to many. But they'd chosen to visit the club, and if those who didn't understand it cut themselves off from the ones who participated... He couldn't concern himself with that.

He swigged the dregs of his coffee. Oliver sat with his eyes closed. Much as Langham wanted to leave him to it, to not interrupt, they had to get back to the club.

"Oliver?"

Oliver opened his eyes and stared down at his hand. "Oh. It's gone."

"What has?"

"The number."

Langham had obviously pulled him out from somewhere, from the middle of a vision. He

70

regretted calling his name now and cursed himself for being so impatient. It was difficult to balance the two—working to spec as a detective and working alongside Oliver, who only managed to get the clues the spirits decided he could have.

"The number?" Langham asked.

"From what I can gather, he'll kill again on Saturday. I was given the number nine. It was red." He shuddered. "I got the strong sense when the roulette wheel is spun, it'll land on red—a stabbing—but now I'm wondering whether it just meant the redhead is the one who'll be murdered." He sighed and stood, looking weary right down to his bones. "They're not being very clear this time. Usually the images and info are so sharp. I'm worried it's because I'm tired and I'm not reading things right."

"Any information is better than none. I appreciate whatever you can give me. Listen, I have to go back to the club to oversee things there."

"I should go with you."

"All right, but rest when you need to," Langham said. "This thing you do. It always wears you out."

"I will," Oliver said. "But we have to stop him. I can't rest until he's caught."

The club was a mix of excitement and impatience. In the auditorium, people milled around or talked in huddles, and others sat, either chatting or just staring into space. Those from the main club were questioned, and some were allowed to leave. They hadn't seen anything, hadn't been into the show, and most of them, drunk and incoherent, had been a waste of time.

Those who remained were shepherded into the show room, many also being told they could go home, having seen nothing of importance. Everyone from the front row and five rows behind it remained, being questioned. Officers scribbled in notebooks, SOCO busy in the immediate area surrounding the seat where the killer had sat. It would be a lucky break if any prints were found and matched to someone already in the database, but miracles like that rarely happened, and Langham wasn't banking on winning that particular lottery.

Oliver walked up and down, closing his eyes every so often and pausing to listen. If he got something of major importance, he'd find Langham and let him know. For now, Langham just had to hope that fingerprints or a hair would be found, maybe even fibres from the man's clothes.

He walked over to the techs. "Make sure the chair next to his is checked, the one to its right. Our potential victim was sitting there." If they could find her before... God, he hoped they did. It would take a bit of pressure off, but with only a few days until the next weekend, the chances were they'd fail. It happened so often in his cases, but it didn't stop him wishing for a miracle.

A SOCO lifted something off the killer's chair with tweezers. Langham stepped forward, then went down on his haunches to see what had been found. It was a wad of peach-coloured rubber, knobbly like a mountain and flat on the underside. He frowned, not recognising it as anything he'd seen before.

"What the fuck is that?" he murmured.

The SOCO held it up, turning it around to study it. "No idea. Seems like there's some form of glue on the bottom. On the edges, see?"

Langham narrowed his eyes to get a better look at a crust in one area and a globule of matter in another. "Bloody weird. This is from the killer's seat, yes?"

The tech shook his head. "Wedged between the two. Could have fallen out of a pocket. Might not be anything to do with him if the maintenance staff don't make a habit of cleaning thoroughly. At first I thought it was a bit of chewing gum, but it isn't big enough." He lightly squeezed the tweezers. "And it's too soft. Gum would be harder by now."

"Depends how long ago it was put there," Langham said. "But yep, I think we can rule out gum."

Bagging it, the SOCO then concentrated his efforts between the seats again. "Christ, there's a lot of shit in here. Makes our job harder. The lab's going to be a while on this lot."

Langham sucked his top lip. "And time isn't something we have."

"When do we ever?" the SOCO said.

Langham got up and sighed. The odds of them sorting through the findings before Saturday were slim. Frustrated, he wanted to shout, to punch a wall. He glanced at Oliver, who was in pause mode, his head back, face tilted to the ceiling. He opened his eyes, gaze landing on Langham, as though he'd known exactly where he'd be. It should have unnerved Langham, this ability Oliver had to pick up on things, but he was used to it now. He went to him, cocking his head, raising his eyebrows.

"Anything?" he asked.

"A few things." Oliver nodded absently. "I saw him clearer, as he is without his disguise. He hasn't got a crazed expression, he's just so normal."

"They usually are. Someone you'd never suspect. Look at the amount of people we see coming through the station every day. Like that woman the other week. I never would have taken her for a child beater. You know the one, hair in a bun, a twinset and pearls, for fuck's sake. Like anyone's jolly granny. Yet she'd been hitting the children she supposedly loved caring for. And think about how she didn't deny it, how she didn't see what she'd been doing as wrong. She'd been cleared as a childminder by the authorities, had the certificate and everything, yet she'd managed to hurt so many and not get caught for ages. Who knew a granny could threaten all sorts so the kids didn't tell? The outer package hides a multitude of sins. This man is no different."

"I know. And I wonder how come he hasn't got a girlfriend?"

"How do you know he hasn't?"

"I just know. I don't think he's ever had one. It's like... Like he skipped the usual boy-to-man thing, where going out to get laid is the highlight of your weekend. When I saw him in my head just now, a boatload of information came at me. He's a loner—yes, they usually are, or they at least keep to themselves if they do live with their families. He isn't interested in interacting with anyone—it makes him uncomfortable, and the only reason he's doing it at the club with these women is because it's a means to an end. Or because God has told him to. It seems he can't make his own mind up, that being directed is how he's always lived his life. I also think he's totally unaware of the effect he has on young women. They're flattered someone like him wants to chat them up, and that's in his favour."

"And he's possibly given her the impression he's after a relationship with her..." Langham pursed his lips then shook his head. "And she's fallen for it. Has no idea what he's really up to. Fuck, this shit stinks."

"It does, but what can we do other than what we're already doing? I can't force the spirits to show me anything. I can't promise to interpret the images they're giving me into the correct answer. We just have to guess."

Langham nodded, rubbing his palm over his stubbled chin. "Guesswork. I'm used to that." He

75

thought about the weird piece of rubber the tech had found and told Oliver about it. "Think about that and see if you get anything. I'll leave you be."

"You don't need to," Oliver said. "It's been up his nose."

"What?" Langham frowned. "Why the fuck would it have been up there?"

"It's part of his disguise. I can see him now as he was when he took Tina and Lisa. He wedged it against his septum to make it appear deviated."

"Devious, never mind deviated. The fucking bastard!"

"It'll have DNA on it."

"But that isn't any good if he isn't in the database. He left nothing behind at the scenes." Anger at being powerless swept through him. He wanted to punch a wall again.

"I know, but look at it this way. It'll secure an arrest if it matches any samples taken from him. We have to find the positives, otherwise, what else is there to keep us going? Keep us searching?"

Oliver was right, but it didn't make Langham feel any better. That murdering tosser had been here—*right here*—and he'd walked away, free to do whatever the hell he wanted.

"What did he say his name was? You know, when he introduced himself at the club?" Langham asked, the damn thing on the tip of his tongue. "Jim? Something like that?"

"Joe Adams," Oliver said. "But it's as fake as his looks. Yet another disguise."

"I'll ring that information in. Just in case. You never know."

CHAPTER TEN

The Past

*T*he missing woman was found today. Dead. She'd spoken to Oliver the minute he'd gone near her death site. He'd expected that, but not the fact that she was so...insistent, so pushy in getting through. She was the closest any spirit had ever got to him—her presence was right there, right beside *him, next to him, in him—and he had to take a moment to decide whether to ask her to back off or to just let her remain where she was. He chose the latter, thinking that if she got any closer, he'd put some distance between them.*

He stood beside Langham on the edge of a boggy field, at the fringes of a forest that seemed to stretch ahead for miles, thousands of tree trunks, the light in between them vertical slits of brightness where the sun had managed to sneak through. It was odd, standing there on a glorious, if chilly day, when a body was sprawled at their feet. She was partially clothed—top half intact, light-blue blouse, navy suit jacket, her lower clothes missing, including her shoes. He knew from the CCTV image that she'd had on a beige pencil skirt, the hem just sitting at her knees, and a pair of low-heeled courts that had appeared black. She'd worked as a secretary, and her briefcase was beneath her head, a hard, obscene rendition of a pillow.

What he found hard to swallow was seeing a corpse in the flesh. He had to accept the information that she was there, a shell of what she'd previously been—someone's wife, mother, sister, aunt...

He shut his emotions off and concentrated on what she wanted to say. It wouldn't do the investigation any good if he allowed himself to get upset by the swamping feelings regarding the hole that now gaped in the lives of those she'd left behind. A hole she hadn't dug or expected to be put in.

"He's a bum," *she said.* "A strange little bum I'd seen before but hadn't really taken any notice of. I'd noticed him, yes, hanging around outside the offices where I work, but he hadn't posed a threat. I thought he'd been waiting for a lift, because he was always there after work."

Her words were followed by pictures, and Oliver saw the man as she had on her last day, all waistband hanging halfway down his arse, black baseball cap perched on a head of unruly dark curls. And he was a bum, or at least looked like one, someone who didn't care for his appearance much, or didn't have a lot of money to dress better. But Oliver sensed he had a job, some meaning to his life other than following the woman and grabbing her down an alleyway.

"He brought me here in his car," *she said.* "He'd parked it at the end of the alley. A beat-up Ford Fiesta, red, the paintwork dull, rusty on the front grille and around the rear light casings. He put me in the boot, taped my mouth up, taped my wrists and ankles. Yellow tape. I remember thinking that was it, that I'd never see my husband or kids again, and I was right, wasn't I? I always thought I'd have fought, but something inside told me it was pointless, that I'd be doing a lot of work for no reason. I knew, without a doubt, that I wasn't meant to be here anymore. Sad, that, but there you have it."

Her words had Oliver wanting to shout out his frustration at the unfairness in the world, but he held off, focusing on her body, on the visuals inside his head. *She'd been violated sexually, and the killer had taken her skirt, her shoes, and Oliver saw them on top of a ladder-back chair in a sparsely furnished room. The skirt was folded, the shoes placed side by side on top, and they looked as though she'd be picking them up any moment and getting dressed again.*

The knowledge that she wasn't brought a lump to his throat.

"Just find him," *she said*, "so my husband can move on. He'll not rest until this man's caught."

Oliver could understand that, and also, the spotlight of suspicion might fall on her husband very soon if no leads were found. The spouse was always watched carefully.

He nodded, and suddenly a shift in closeness occurred. The woman's spirit had gone inside him totally, and he felt what she felt—anguish, hatred, desperation—and saw through her eyes. She took him to the boot of the car, and he stared at a serial number etched into the silver rim of the interior light casing. He memorised it, repeating it over and over in his mind until it spewed out of his mouth and had Langham putting his hand on his shoulder.

"What's that?" Langham asked, his voice seeming to come from afar.

Oliver tried to pull away, out of wherever the woman had taken him, but her hold was extreme. "Let me go," *he told her calmly.* "I can't help you if you persist in keeping me here like this."

"What?" Langham asked. "I'm not keeping you anywhere."

Oliver shook his head, trying to make him understand he hadn't meant him. "Her." He nodded at her body. "She's too close. Inside me."

"How do you get her out?" Langham asked, panic in his voice.

"I'll... I'll have to close her off completely, and if I do that, she might not come back. Quickly, write down the number I just gave you."

The sound of fumbling—probably him reaching for his notebook—then, "Shit! Go on."

Oliver repeated it several times. "Got it?"

"Yes. What is it?"

"I'll explain in a minute. I need to... God, I need to get her out of me."

She faded a little, as though she wasn't quite sure whether to leave him or not.

"Go on," Oliver encouraged. "I promise I'll help you."

"I can't go," *she said.* "What if this is the only time I can get through? What if I go somewhere else and I'm stuck? My babies, my Jack, I need... I have to do this for them..."

"I understand." God, she was making him so tired, sucking out his energy. "I can't do this if you stay. Go. Now."

He hated himself for being so harsh, but what he'd said was true. He'd be next to useless for many hours if she didn't release her hold. He channelled on her presence, mentally pushing her away, imagining himself gently shoving at her chest. She clung on, a desperate woman, her fingertips the only thing holding her to the edge of a cliff, then she was falling, heading towards blackness he could only imagine was purgatory. He jolted, her body on the sodden grass coming into stark reality.

"Jesus Christ," Langham said. "Are you all right?"

"I will be. Just give me a minute." A pause. "That number. You need to—"

"Already been done. Someone should get back to me soon. We'll find him."

Two hours later, the car was found abandoned, and after a computer check, it was discovered the last owner had filed that it had been stolen. Of course, he was questioned—it could have been him after all—but Oliver walked past an interview room and glanced through the small window in the top of the door and knew it wasn't him. He let Langham know, then went to see Sue, the artist, who drew a very good likeness of the man Oliver saw in his head.

Someone had to know him, would recognise him. And maybe they would once that image was plastered all over the national newspapers and on TV.

Early forensic reports had come in that the killer had been very careful—no clear footprints embedded in the wet mud surrounding her body— and it had been surmised that he'd covered his shoes or boots with some sort of foam then overlaid that with plastic bags. No tread visible, just a shape that resembled a foot. So he'd known what he was going to do, had planned it well, and when caught wouldn't be treated lightly. Premeditation got Langham's team's backs up.

The man had also sexually abused her without penile penetration—no signs of semen or a condom being used—but there were indications he'd used something inside her, again, possibly encased in a bag. Did the bags have some significance for him, as he'd killed her by using a plastic bag over her head, too? He'd tightened and tied it around her neck, the individual ridges of the bunched-up noose clearly visible on her skin. The circle of the knot, too, a dark bruise marring the hollow of her neck.

Awful. Just bloody awful.

CHAPTER ELEVEN

He had gone home. Without any weeding to do, no housework, he was at a loss. He was antsy, felt the need to do something, but he wasn't sure what. Maybe a visit to the abandoned house would work out the kinks, make him sleepy. He was so wired at the moment that going to bed wasn't an option. Tossing and turning, staring at the ceiling wasn't what he classed as fruitful when he could be elsewhere, doing something productive.

He left his house to return to his car then pulled away from the kerb, pretty pleased with how the night had gone. The redhead had got on his nerves just like the other two, but it was a price he'd had to pay to carry out God's wishes, a price he'd continue to pay for as long as He wanted him.

His journey to the abandoned house swept by almost without his notice, and he parked in his usual spot so his car was hidden. He went inside, going straight upstairs to the bedroom where he'd taken the other two women. Something wasn't right. He looked around, frowning, unable to figure out what. There it was—spots of blood on the floorboards and a hank of Tina's hair where she'd pulled it out once the pain had become too much.

He shook his head. Some people just didn't know how to behave.

In the kitchen, he took out his cleaning gear, then a bucket from the cupboard under the sink, which he filled to the halfway point—amazingly, the water hadn't been cut off. Back in the bedroom, he went down on hands and knees and stuffed the hair into his jeans pocket. With that out of the way, he sprayed bathroom cleaner and used a scrubbing brush to try to get rid of the stains. They wouldn't budge—they faded, but that stubborn redness refused to be lifted. It had soaked into the boards. Why hadn't he cleaned it properly after he'd loaded the angels into the boot of his car?

He thought back. It had been because the second woman had taken longer to die—no consideration for his schedule whatsoever—and he'd needed to take them home before the sun came up.

He mustn't make such a mistake again. Not cleaning up properly could have dire consequences. Not only had he left behind evidence that they'd been killed there, but for all he knew there were clues about him, too. He stormed outside to his car, annoyed with himself for being so careless in not putting on his boiler suit prior to going inside. Taking it from the boot, he dressed within the cover of the bushes. After, he snapped on some latex gloves. Put on a paper hat, much like a shower cap, and locked the car. He entered the house, determined to do things the right way this time.

It took a while, maybe an hour or so, but he finished his scrub of the rooms he'd been in, satisfied that anything he'd left behind was now gone. Those forensic people were very thorough and could find even the most microscopic piece of evidence, but bar burning the house down, there wasn't much else he could do.

God spoke to him, saying he had done enough, and he left the house feeling ten times better. Once he'd undressed in the bushes, he placed his things back in the boot then sat in the driver's seat. Thought back to his first attempt at killing some time ago and how wrong it had gone. He'd been too conscious of using plastic—had worn gloves, had strangled her with a black refuse sack that he'd fashioned into a tight noose by twisting it— and he hadn't felt right about her death at all. He knew now, after conversing with God, that he'd misinterpreted His instructions.

Then it hit him. He'd made yet another mistake with the last two. His first abduction... He'd put her in his car boot, and traces of her were probably still there. Had possibly stuck to his boiler suit, and him going back into the house to clean it—Lord, her hairs or fibres could very well be in there now.

He shook his head. Saw an image of her in his mind. She babbled about her husband, Jack, and her brats. She'd been different from the last two, though. She hadn't fought. Had accepted what he was going to do. It was just a shame that he'd done what many other killers did and penetrated her sexually. And where had he put her skirt and shoes?

He couldn't remember.

That didn't sit too well. He'd have to be more astute in future. Mistakes might lead to him being caught.

Still wide awake, he stared at the foliage around him and tried to think of something else he could do tonight other than rehashing the past. He didn't have the annoying issue of work to think about— he was on Jobseeker's Allowance at the moment and pretended week after week that he'd applied for jobs and just hadn't got them. There was no time for toiling when he had another kind of job to do, so if he didn't make it to bed at a reasonable hour, it didn't matter.

"I'll go back to the club," he murmured, starting the engine and heading that way. If the redhead cancelled on him, he really should have another ready to take her place.

He parked down the same side street, annoyed that his previous space by the unlit streetlamp had been stolen by someone else. What was it with folks these days? No respect, that was what it was, no thought for others. He had to walk another few yards because of someone else's thoughtlessness, and by the time he reached the club he was more than a little annoyed. There was no queue—unusual, there was always a long line at this time of night—so he strode straight up to a bouncer guarding the door. He frowned at no music filtering out. The bouncer didn't step aside to let him in and, impatient with his behaviour, he stifled the urge to lash out.

"Closed, mate," the bouncer said.

"Closed?"

"Police matter." He puffed his chest out.

"Oh, is everything all right?" Scenarios went through his mind. Had the torture scene turned nasty? Had someone started a fight?

The doorman looked at him, expression serious. "May as well tell you. Probably be all over the news tomorrow anyway." After a nod he went on, leaning forward to say, "They're searching for that bloke who killed those women."

His stomach churned. "What would he be doing in there?"

"Dunno. They got a tip-off he'd been in tonight, apparently. There's other evidence that says he picked the women up from here last week. That he'd chosen another one earlier on this evening. Checking the CCTV and all sorts, they are."

The mention of the cameras set his teeth on edge. And here he stood, right at the door where one of the cameras was trained. He swore inside his head, waiting for God to tell him everything would be all right.

Nothing came, not even the faintest whisper.

"Bloody hell," he said, trying to act casual, his heart rate accelerating. "You just never know, do you? Are you opening again in a bit?"

"Nah, closed for the rest of the night now, mate."

"Shit. I wanted a drink an' all."

"Try Cleaver's down the road a bit. Open till three like we usually are."

Cleaver. Maybe he'd buy one to use on the redhead.

"Ah, right. Thanks."

He walked away, stifling the desire to run, but he couldn't be doing with getting caught for acting suspiciously.

I'll go home where I'm safe. No one will find me there.

Oliver had tried and failed to get any more information. He'd left the auditorium with Langham, and they were now in a small office upstairs, a bank of CCTV screens on the desk in front of them. A brunette woman of about twenty-four—Joy, she'd said her name was—sat scanning a CD for the time just before the auditorium had been opened to admit spectators.

Oliver and Langham stood behind her, Langham propping himself on the desk with one hand, leaning over Joy's shoulder. The camera footage pointed at the door at the top of the stairs, although the rest of the auditorium below was still in view.

Oliver held his breath, waiting for the door to open. Joy had it on fast-forward, and a man came in and walked down the steps with the waddle of Charlie Chaplin.

"Stop!" Oliver said.

Langham echoed it a second later.

With the footage rewound, Oliver leant closer, Joy's hair tickling his chin, and peered at the grainy film. He'd have thought with today's technology it would have been clearer, in colour, too, but it was black and white, a murky scene owing to the lights being turned down low. It was *him*, Oliver recognised his clothes, and he went down the stairs, glancing around him as though checking to see if anyone else was about. Oliver clenched his teeth, so annoyed with himself for not realising who he was when he'd spoken to them.

"We had him." He shook his head. "Bloody *had* him!"

"These things happen," Langham said. "If you didn't do what you did, we wouldn't even be here. There's no way we'd have found out so soon that he trawls this place for women."

Joy, pretty but weary-looking, shivered. "Bloody makes me feel sick to think of someone like that in here."

"I know what you mean." Oliver eyed the screen. "So he came alone. Oh, hang on. The door's opening again."

A small crowd of women came in. One of them made her way down the steps and sat beside the man. They'd clearly met before.

"Any way to zoom in on this?" Langham asked.

"Which bit?" Joy said.

"The women. They could be crucial," he said.

Joy pressed a button and enlarged the screen. "That enough?"

"No, I need it closer. Just their faces." Langham pressed his fingertips onto the desk. Leant forward a bit more. "That's it. Pause it." He glanced over Joy's head at Oliver. "This could be the break we need." To Joy, he said, "Can you print a still of this?"

"Yep, give me a second."

While she got up and moved to a printer in the corner, Oliver studied the faces on the monitor. "One of those women was still downstairs when we came up here, I'm sure of it. That one there." He pointed to lady with light hair. "Did you see her? She was sitting a little way along from the killer's seat."

"Shit," Langham said. "Better get a move on in case she's been told she can go home."

"Here you go." Joy turned from the printer then walked towards them, picture held out. "Sorry it isn't very clear."

"No worries." Langham took the image and turned it into a scroll. "And thanks for all your help. If you could make a copy of that footage—an officer will collect it shortly—and if you find any more of that man leaving with a woman, get hold of me or another officer. Actually, I'll send someone up to sit with you. Four eyes are better than two and all that."

Oliver followed him back downstairs, his inner voice screaming that they needed to hurry. "Quickly," he said, heart hammering.

They entered the main nightclub area from the back, through a door beside the one that led to the auditorium. A spirit shrieked at him, the noise hurting his ears. He covered them, knowing it was pointless—the sound was in his head—then lowered his hands to his sides. He caught sight of someone in similar clothes to the light-haired woman in the picture, and the spirit keened again, obviously unable to form words.

"Wait!" he shouted.

The woman turned and looked at Oliver— barely eighteen if her baby face was any indication, perhaps younger—and Oliver went to her, Langham close behind. Oliver got the sense she was scared, that she shouldn't even have been allowed inside.

Langham unrolled the paper and held it up. "Is this you?"

She nodded, eyes wide, her heartbeat thundering through Oliver.

Oh God, the blonde thought. *I'm so in shit if I get caught being in here.*

"We're not interested in your age," Oliver said, smiling.

The blonde's relief was evident by the slumping of her shoulders, then the thought, *Shit. Shit, how did they know? Dad's going to go mad.*

"Who else were you with?" Langham asked. "Are they still here?"

She shook her head, a frantic side-to-side that moved her hair, the ends writhing on her shoulders like worms. "No."

"The redhead," Oliver said calmly. He put one hand on the girl's arm. "Where is she?"

"I don't know. She left ages ago with some bloke she'd met here before."

"I need her name and address." Langham pulled out his notebook.

A huge spirit sigh rippled inside Oliver's head, and he relaxed his shoulders, tension seeping out of him. The girl gave the information they needed, and Langham also took hers.

"I might need to contact you again," he said. "You've been very helpful."

"But my dad..." She glanced from Langham to Oliver.

"Hopefully he won't need to know anything," Oliver said. "But if he does... It's for your friend's sake. You being here is just something you'll have to admit to, I'm afraid, love."

"Is my friend all right? Has she done anything wrong?" She wrung her hands.

"No," Oliver said. "She's absolutely fine."

Please let that be the truth. Please don't let him have taken her already.

CHAPTER TWELVE

Langham drove through the streets with ease, the lack of traffic at this time of night a far cry from what it would have been had they been on their way to the redhead's by day. His blood was up, adrenaline flowing through him, and with Oliver by his side he was sure they'd pick up more clues once they reached their destination. Another detective and uniformed officers were on standby in case Langham needed them, but he felt he could deal with this by himself for now—unless the killer bastard was still there.

"You all right?" he asked Oliver, hopeful, as usual, that he was already getting information.

"Silence," he said, "although there's a sense of... I get the feeling the killer isn't there."

"What about her?" He swerved around a parked car then took a left.

"She's there. Alone."

"Good. But is she...?"

"I don't know. I'm not getting anything on whether she's alive or dead. It's like someone's waiting, a spirit, to get through, but their way is blocked by another force."

"A bad one?"

"No, just... A shield of some sort. I don't understand it."

"Maybe the spirits just can't get through," Langham said. "That shield might be them unable to speak to you, their way of letting you know they're waiting. For you to be on the alert for when they *can* manage to speak."

"It's possible. I've given up trying to work it all out. I mean, what started off as limited information has escalated to full-on psychic shit. I'm still trying to come to grips with that, but at the same time I've been telling myself to go with it. Like, if I think about it too much it'll block information, not make it come faster, make sense?"

"Yep." Langham took a right. "So do it. Don't analyse, even though you're a fucker for doing that. It's who you are, after all."

"Yeah, well, I reckon it's time I changed that. It can only help."

Another right had Langham's gut rolling. "We're in her street. I'll drive past her place first, see if any lights are on, see what cars are outside. If his is there, a Ford... Going to have to call for backup."

"Good. I don't much fancy bursting in on them without help. I know you could handle it, but... I don't want to risk anything."

"I won't be risking fuck all." He drove towards the redhead's house. "See his car anywhere, or at least the same type?"

Oliver leant forward, stared out of the windscreen. "Nope. He isn't here, I know he isn't. I've got glimpses of her in my head. She's inside, on a dark-green leather sofa. Mint-green throw pillows on it."

"Right. Good." Langham pulled up to the kerb, parked, then shut off the engine. Looked across at Oliver. "And even though I've seen time and again that what you get in your head is what I'll see when I go inside people's houses, it still shits me up that you were right."

Oliver laughed. "Imagine how I used to feel as a kid then. When I didn't understand all this stuff. I used to think I'd been there before and just didn't remember it. Come on. We need to get inside. Warn her."

Langham sighed. "Yep. Not something I'm looking forward to, I must say."

"Me neither. Wonder if she's prone to hysterics?"

Langham shook his head. "Is that solid information or just you literally wondering? Any warning that she's going to freak out on me would be appreciated."

"Just me wondering. Besides, if I tell you everything, it kind of takes the edge off your work." Oliver grinned. "Won't hurt for you to have the element of surprise every now and then."

"Fucker." Langham chuckled as he got out of the car and stood on the path, staring at the house and its surroundings.

She lived in a small, detached, red-brick effort, a narrow alleyway either side, ones he assumed led to the back gardens of all the homes in the row. A blue recycle wheelie bin stood to the right, the lid open a bit, rubbish—a Pepsi bottle and the corner of a Domino's takeaway pizza box—poking out. There weren't front gardens as such, just a communal lawn broken by paved paths leading up to the front doors. The killer would have his work cut out for him on this one—with him parking at the kerb, and the depth of the lawn, he risked someone seeing him either abducting her or bringing her back to place her inside once he'd killed her.

"What do you reckon?" Langham glanced at Oliver beside him.

"He'll have to return here after killing, later, like in the middle of the night so he isn't seen."

"I thought the same. And he's been clever. Chosen a place where there are no adjoining walls. Less chance of any neighbours hearing him letting himself in. Hopefully it won't come to that." He grimaced.

"Hopefully she's alive…"

"Only one way to find out."

Langham rolled his shoulders and led the way up her path. He knocked on the door, stomach in knots that they might not get a reply. She could be the type to leave lights on overnight—living alone, she may have thought it would deter intruders. She might not hear his knocking. He gave Oliver a sidelong look, received a nod to try again and did so, hitting the wood harder this time, sharp pain streaking across his knuckles.

A shadow appeared at what he assumed was the end of a hallway, the shape of someone peering around a doorjamb. The figure then moved to stand in the centre of the doorway, shrouded by pale-yellow light, and drew closer. Langham swallowed, smoothed his jacket sleeves, then took out his identification. The door swung ajar on quiet hinges, and the redhead poked her face into the small gap.

"Yes?" she asked, frowning, then smiling as she recognised them. "Oh, it's you. From the club. How did you know…?"

"Detective Langham." He showed her his badge. "And my assistant, Oliver Banks. May we come in?"

She widened her eyes, lifted one hand to loiter her fingers at the base of her throat, then stepped back, opening the door some more. "I suppose… Have I done something wrong?" She completely moved away, backed into the hall, and allowed them to come in.

"Not in the sense you might be thinking." Claustrophobia zoomed in on Langham in the narrow space, even more so after Oliver closed the door and all three of them were cramped there. "Is there somewhere we can talk?"

"Yes." She frowned again. "Through here."

She went down the hall and turned right. Langham followed, Oliver at his rear, and glanced in at a living room with a green sofa and mint throw pillows. He shuddered and entered the room she'd gone into. She stood beside a small pine kitchen table that had four spindle-backed chairs wedged around it.

"Would you like a drink?" She went towards a worktop under a window where there was a kettle and mug tree beside a stainless-steel sink.

"I wouldn't mind a coffee," Langham said. "Thank you."

She looked at Oliver.

"Same for me, thanks," he said.

"Do you want to sit down?" she asked.

Langham nodded, and as she put the kettle on to boil, he and Oliver pulled out a chair each and sat.

"So, um, what's going on?" She spooned instant coffee into three cups. "I mean, if I've done something, I'm not aware of it. And it must have been at the club because you were there…"

"You haven't done anything illegal," Langham said. "We just need to ask you a couple of questions about the man you were with—how you met him, when you're seeing him again—and also to explain some things to you."

"Oh, right. Well, that's okay then. I thought… Well, I thought the club and what went on there wasn't legal or something and that by just being there I was in the sh— In trouble." She laughed unsteadily.

"No, no, nothing like that." Langham smiled.

She brought their drinks over, put them directly on the table, ignoring the pile of coasters in the middle. Langham did the honours, dealing the coasters out like thick black cards, aces of hearts, a single red symbol of love in the centre of them. She collected her coffee then sat, placed her hands in her lap, and waited.

Langham took a sip. Burnt his tongue. "Lovely. Thank you. Now, the man you were with…"

"Joe Adams?" she asked. "He's… Well, he's just some bloke I met the other week. He talks to lots of women—don't think he wants a full-on relationship with anyone, he's more your go-out-on-dates-every-so-often type, know the kind I mean?"

Langham nodded.

"Well. Joe. He's... He's all right, if you get me. He's just a bloke. I could see myself being with him, quite fancy exclusive dates and whatnot"— she blushed—"but I don't think he's into me like that. Not really."

"I see." Langham took another sip, aware of Oliver observing her in a way that she wouldn't know he was reading her body language. "So when are you meeting next?"

"Oh, he invited me to some fancy dress party. *Not* that I'm into *that* either, but it might be fun. You know, wear something you wouldn't normally. Become a different person for the night. Quite fancied being Wonder Woman, something like that, but he suggested me being an angel. So how come you need to know things about him? Is he...like is he a criminal or something?"

"You could say that." Langham shifted in his seat a bit. Looked her directly in the eye. "We have reason to believe he's killed two women—possibly more that we're not aware of."

"What?" she shrieked, scraping her chair back and standing, hands to her chest, her face going white. "Are you fucking serious? Oh my God. Oh my fucking God!"

"Please, sit down. I know this must be difficult to take in but—"

"Difficult to take in?" She danced from foot to foot, appearing as though she contemplated fight or flight. "He's been in my bloody house! He's touched me! Oh God..." She stopped moving, shuddered, and closed her eyes, only to snap them

106

open again and stare at Langham with what must have been glassy vision. "Will he come back? I mean, am I...?"

"Sit down. Please, just sit down." Langham half stood, reaching out a hand across the table, waving it to coax her back to her seat. "That's it. Just for a moment. Take a few deep breaths."

She did, closing her eyes again. A plethora of emotions scurried across her face. Acute fear was at the top of the list. Sweat broke out on her forehead and at her temples, and she drew her mouth into a tight moue, the lines around her lips standing out, burgundy slashes against the surrounding whiteness. When she opened her eyes, he continued.

"We think you may be next on his list. Now then"—he put his hand on top of one of hers—"we don't know that for sure. What I need is for you to give me any information you can about him, however small, however insignificant you might think it is. For example, any numbers or letters from his licence plate. The exact colour and make of his car. Whether he's let slip anything about where he lives, what he does for a living, things like that." He fished in his pocket for a notebook. "Just take your time, relax, and as you recall things, I'll write them down. If you need to stop and take five at any point, do so."

"But what will I do?" She curled the hand beneath his into a fist. "What the fuck am I meant to do? He might come here. He might break in and get me. Oh shit, he might... He knows where I work, everything!"

"We'll get to that," Langham said. "And you'll be safe at all times, I promise. But for now, we just need you to remember. Start from the beginning, from the first time you ever saw him. Then move on through your memories until the present time. All right?"

She blew out a breath, nodding, staring at the steam rising from her cup, but he'd bet she wasn't seeing it.

"All right. Shit, all right," she said.

She went through the lot, which ended up with Langham filling several pages of his notebook. He drove a battered red Ford Fiesta. Oliver disappeared into the hallway when she mentioned that to relay the information to the station. Once she'd finished, Langham smiled at her and asked Oliver to make them another cuppa.

"Now," Langham said. "This is what happens next. I don't think he's going to do anything on Friday night, but I can't be certain of that." He glanced at Oliver. "If he does what we think he'll do, he'll keep you out until midnight comes, as we have information that he's planning his next attack on Saturday the ninth. I have a plan, something I'll need your cooperation with, and if you're up for helping us out, I'll let you know what you need to do."

CHAPTER THIRTEEN

That business at the club had really annoyed him. Something wasn't right, but he couldn't put his finger on it. Apart from the obvious—the police being there and whatever—there was something else nagging at him, speaking in tongues he couldn't understand.

He paced his living room, going through the evening from start to finish. He'd been meticulous in covering his tracks, in making sure everything had been done just so, yet the police had known he'd chosen women from Chains. Maybe because the two women he'd bumped off recently had a past together—was that it? Had they known one another? It hadn't seemed like it when he'd collected them. Perhaps their movements prior to death had been looked into. Yes, that must have been what had happened. The police had realised they'd both frequented the same club and had put two and two together. But who had known he'd been there tonight? He'd certainly not told anyone of his important job, what he'd been selected to do—so really, his identity ought to still be secure.

Maybe he'd underestimated the police.

No maybe about it. Lord, please tell me what I must do next. I mustn't get caught if I'm to continue to do what you request of me. The next one must be a red number, I know that, and she's all excited, looking forward to us going out. Do I carry on with your mission?

He received no answer and, feeling vulnerable and abandoned, he went into the hallway to peer at himself in the mirror. His face was his. No disguise. No extra piece inside his nose. No fake facial hair. What had he been thinking, going out on the prowl like this? Had he become so sure of his work, God's orders, that he'd imagined himself invincible or that God would protect him whether people interfered or not?

110

No, God couldn't control the actions of other humans, only him.

But You could have given me a warning.

Silence.

Perhaps he had been given one and he just hadn't seen it. Too busy being wrapped up in what he was doing instead of taking care to think about the finer details, the small slip-ups. Take tonight, for instance. He'd had to return to the old house and clear up the mess—mess he should have cleaned the night he'd killed them.

He wouldn't be making such an error again. No, he'd take great care to ensure that on Friday night he was on the ball, in top form. If he wasn't, he had a very frightening feeling that he may well get caught.

CHAPTER FOURTEEN

Oliver sat opposite Langham at a table in the corner of the station canteen. His office had become claustrophobic. Eating lunch in there as well as sifting through the club's CCTV footage all morning hadn't appealed. Oliver was tired, getting a bit antsy, pissed off, too, and Langham appeared to be suffering much the same.

"This Joe bloke," Oliver said. "I knew the name was fake." News had come in that the two Joe Adamses in the city were both old and had alibis. "Wonder whether it has some significance for him."

"It's possible." Langham took a sip of tea. "And him giving his victims a fake one when he introduces himself... Sensible. I mean, you don't want to be giving out your real one, especially if it's unusual."

"I s'pose. And we're still left with a couple of thousand cars, even though they've been narrowed down with the redhead's information. Too many people to visit and question before Friday, I take it?"

"Yes, and alerting him before then... Counterproductive when we've got plans in place."

"You reckon it'll work?" Oliver stirred his tea, more for something to do than anything. "I mean, what if he's watching her? What if he clocks the surveillance coppers in that van or the unmarked car this week? Won't it put him off?"

Langham shrugged. "Who can say? He might well imagine he's going to get away with it scot-free. Why would he think she's being watched? Why would he think she'd have the police waiting inside her place when he goes to pick her up?"

Oliver frowned. "I don't know, I just... I reckon he knows."

114

"Did you get told that outright or is it just you sensing it?"

"Sensing. If I think about him, remember what he looks like, I kind of get impressions. I can't get a handle on him exactly, just wafts of information, insubstantial at that. He at least realises the police know of him—not that he is who he is, but that he's been to the club and whatever, that the net is closing. He doesn't seem to understand why." Oliver closed his eyes and concentrated. "Yeah, he's confused about things. How he's been sent on a 'mission' that might fail—confused about why he's been chosen to do what he's doing if whoever is sending him knows it'll go wrong." Oliver shivered. "He feels let down. His contact isn't answering his questions."

"Interesting." Langham dragged a tea plate towards him then lifted a croissant from it, tugging off one of the ends. "So this is possibly a team?"

"No, he's acting alone."

"Then I don't get what you're saying—you mentioned a contact."

"I don't get it either. Someone's telling him what to do, yet at the same time he's doing it by himself. The God thing for sure."

"Ah, I'm with you. Of course God isn't going to answer him. I doubt very much the Almighty ever spoke to him in the first bloody place."

A wave of information floated through Oliver's mind so quickly he almost didn't catch it. "He's definitely going to go ahead on Friday, picking her up for the fancy dress party and whatnot. Then after midnight he'll try for the red version. The stabbing. But he's worried she won't choose the right number."

"Jesus Christ. This is so far beyond fucked up. I always think I've seen or heard it all, then someone like him comes along and proves me wrong."

"It's a nasty business, this."

Langham nodded. "You're telling me." He stuffed the croissant end into his mouth. Chewed then swallowed. "Do you ever regret what you do?"

"Not really, no. I could do without all the macabre shit, seeing them not only in my head but for real as well, but then again, I wouldn't have it any other way. It's what I do. What I'm meant to be doing. Like you feel about what you do."

"I'm thinking of taking a break," Langham said. "We'll get this case out of the way, then I'll put in for some leave. Fancy a lads' holiday?"

"Yeah," Oliver said. "You've twisted my arm."

A two-tone bell *donged* out of the overhead speaker. "Would Detective Langham come to the front desk, please, thank you."

Oliver froze. Waited for a spinning penny to drop inside his mind. "He's contacted her."

"Who? What?" Langham rose out of his seat.

"Joe. He rang her, said he wanted to meet her tonight. She's here." Oliver got up and followed Langham from the canteen.

116

"Fuck. Bloody fuck it," Langham said over his shoulder. "Just our luck that he'll balls it up now we have everything in place for Friday."

"He's confused about it." Oliver frowned, waiting for the information to settle. "But he's pleased because he finally got an answer to one of his questions."

"And what question was that?" Langham strode towards the double doors that led to the front desk.

"I don't know, but I think the redhead does."

Langham pushed the doors open and held on to one so Oliver could go through. The redhead, Sylvia Hallows, sat in the waiting room. She glanced up at their approach, a smile of relief bleeding onto her face. She stood, lifted her hands in a gesture that screamed 'help', then dropped them to her sides.

"Are you all right?" Langham put a hand on her shoulder.

"Yes. No..." Her cheeks coloured.

"Come with us." Langham guided her to the double doors.

They made their way to his office, and once Langham had offered her a seat and closed the door, he wheeled his desk chair out and put it in front of hers. Sat so he bent forward, clasping her hands in his.

"What's happened?" he asked.

Oliver stayed by the door, leaning on the jamb, trying to get inside her head.

He's coming for me. Oh, God, he's coming for me. He knows. He knows something's wrong, she thought. She repeated much the same, her speech fast, words tumbling over one another.

"Calm down now." Langham smoothed a thumb pad over the back of her hand. "You're fine. You've had officers outside your house twenty-four-seven, remember? If he comes to your home, we'll know about it."

"But he doesn't want to come to my house. He wants me to meet him tonight at some out-of-the-way café down Broad Street. I don't want to go, didn't know what to say about it either, and he pushed, went on and on about it, saying he had to see me, that he hadn't been able to stop thinking about me. I knew it was all bullshit, that what he'd really meant was that he couldn't stop thinking about killing me, but I couldn't say that, could I? I mean, I stayed calm and everything, just said I didn't think I'd be able to make it out tonight, but he insisted, even when I said I had a headache. Then he said…" She paused to take a large breath. "Then he asked what was wrong, that I didn't sound right. Shit, he knows, doesn't he?"

"I don't see how he can, unless he's very vigilant and he's seen officers sitting in their cars in your street—which means he has to have been there." Langham bit his bottom lip, then went on, "But Oliver has information that suggests he's confused about something, and that's probably what's set him off. He's panicking, wondering whether he ought to wait until Friday or get to you earlier, I

118

suspect." He glanced at his watch. "I doubt we have the time to set up such a big operation for tonight, but if he's just wanting you to meet him at a café, I don't see why me and Oliver can't go. Sit at the back and watch."

"But he'll recognise you," she said. "He spoke to you in the club."

"There is that." Langham nodded. "Then we'll play him at his own game."

She frowned. "I don't know what you mean."

"We'll wear a disguise."

CHAPTER FIFTEEN

Far from feeling safer and less like himself, the disguise had Oliver thinking he stood out more. A blaring beacon, that was what he was, and he might as well have yelled his name and what he was doing sitting at the back of a greasy café with Langham, who was in a similar get-up. Both had full beards, wigs, and coloured contacts. The only difference between them was that Langham sported a pair of specs, the thickness of the black frames ensuring he got more than a look or two from other patrons. Still, Joe Adams had only glanced their way briefly, giving them nothing more than a quick once-over, studying everyone else with more intent.

Joe had positioned himself by the window, arriving a few minutes after Oliver and Langham. Oliver had casually watched him go up to the counter and order a coffee and, if Joe had tried to act inconspicuous, he hadn't tried hard enough. He'd been jittery, on edge, and Oliver supposed he would be now. If he suspected something was going on, that he was being watched, he'd be on the alert. Still, he clearly wasn't as professional as Oliver and Langham had first thought. Yes, he'd been meticulous with the forensics side of it— apart from dropping his nose piece down the side of the chair in the show room—but just because he had that area covered, didn't mean he wouldn't fuck up elsewhere.

Oliver concentrated on acting normal, like any other person who'd dropped into a café for a cuppa. The thing was, it wasn't as easy as it sounded. He was on edge himself, worried that things would go tits up and Joe would end up taking Sylvia Hallows and disappearing before they got the chance to follow. Things didn't always go to plan, and although a couple of plain-clothed officers were also outside, smoking while leaning on a lamppost, seeing to be having a fine old time doing it, shit did and could hit the fan in situations like these.

Nervous wasn't the word.

"Nice tea." Langham nodded at his cup and lifted it to his mouth. He held it midair, watching Joe over the rim. "Always gets me how it tastes different in these places. Never could get the same taste at home. Must be the tea bags they use."

Oliver glanced at him. How the hell could he remain so calm? "Don't know. Hadn't really thought about it." He trained his gaze back in Joe's area, staring through the window at the coppers outside but keeping their target in his peripheral.

"He's going to cotton on if you keep watching him like that," Langham whispered. "Pretend he isn't there. We've got him covered."

Oliver turned to Langham, who jerked his head to his right. Oliver followed his gesture. Sergeant Villier was in the far corner. She looked odd out of uniform, didn't seem right without her black trousers, white short-sleeved shirt, and tie. Some detective Oliver would make—he hadn't even realised she was there. Relaxing a bit, yet annoyed with himself that he hadn't picked up on her presence, he leant back against the wall.

"What's the plan?" he asked quietly, even though Joe was too far away to hear him. "I mean, we have no evidence, nothing to really suggest it's him. You can't just arrest him for having a coffee. And without any DNA proof off that fake septum yet, we've got nothing but suspicion and the word

123

of Sylvia that he's invited her to a fancy dress party, know what I mean?"

"That's where the word 'suspicion' comes in handy. You hear it on the news all the time, don't you, people arrested on suspicion of murder. Most of those arrests come from the faintest of evidence. They usually break when we bring them in, thinking we have more on them than we do."

"Bet he doesn't break." Oliver peered at Joe. "Then again, going by the state of him, maybe he will."

Joe fannied about with a napkin, screwing it up then flattening it out, repeating the motion over and over as if it were the only thing keeping him sane. He appeared far from that, though. Eyes wide, mouth pursed, cheeks flushed—no, he didn't seem like the hardened, well-ordered killer they'd supposed he was. What the hell had happened to make him like this? For the life of him, Oliver couldn't imagine this bloke having the confidence to do what he'd done. And those thoughts of his that he'd heard in the show room had given Oliver the impression the man was careful, on the ball, and full of self-assurance.

Something had definitely set him off along the worry track.

Oliver reached out, searching for Joe's subconscious, pushing until he found it, and wedged himself inside the man's mind. Joe gave a jolt and frowned, as though he knew something had happened, then shrugged. He peered around the café. Oliver turned away so he didn't get

124

caught staring and fiddled with the teaspoon resting on his saucer.

She'd better hurry up, Joe thought. *I have to sort this out tonight. She's off. Weird.*

"Oh fuck," Oliver murmured. "She was right. He does know."

"Christ," Langham whispered, taking a sip of his tea, swallowing audibly and putting his cup down. "You in his head or what?"

"Something like that."

Langham nodded. "I'll leave you be then."

Oliver watched the scenes playing out in Joe's head, brought up incredibly short when he saw a woman he'd last seen sprawled out dead on the grass, her skirt and shoes missing, her voice in his head telling him that her Jack wouldn't rest until her killer had been caught.

"Fuck me." Oliver resisted the urge to get the hell up, go over there, and smack the shit out of Joe.

"What?" Langham shifted in his seat. "Do I need to be on the move?"

"Not yet. I'm just watching stuff that he's thinking about. Remember that case we couldn't solve when I first joined your team? That bloke who waited outside that shop for a woman—can't remember her name—and abducted her, killed her with a twisted black rubbish bag? Shit, what was her name?"

"I can't remember either, but go on. Although I have a funny feeling I know what you're going to say."

125

"It was him. She was his first."

Langham released a long sigh through pursed lips. "Right. Anything else?"

Oliver watched some more. Joe outside Chains, waiting in the queue to go inside. Tina and Lisa in front of him, giggling, glancing back at him, typical girls on a night out who'd spotted someone they fancied. Christ, if only the clock could be turned back. They'd damn well been happy, young, and without a care in the world. Joe seemed to be examining the differences among the women, asking himself why his first kill had felt so wrong. Then the image of a roulette wheel filled his mind, that hellish ball bearing prancing around, jumping from number to number as the spin got faster. Joe relaxed then, and Oliver realised that the wheel was what made Joe understand why the bin-bag murder hadn't been right. He hadn't used the wheel.

Joe's thoughts surfaced. *But God didn't tell me I should use it right from the start. Lord, I don't wish to assign blame, but You didn't give me all the tools from the very beginning. You let me kill that woman without the red or black. Was that a test, to see if I'd actually kill someone for You? Yes, that was it. You're so clever.*

Oliver frowned at the man's thinking. He was mad, that much was certain. A shiver went up Oliver's spine, and he caught himself just in time so he didn't shudder.

"Definitely going to blame God," Oliver said.

"Right. Another one for a mental institution instead of prison then." Langham gave a gruff chuckle. "Fucking typical. The worst ones, those who need a dose of the harshness of being jailed with the hard nuts, never seem to get their just deserts."

"You can only do so much," Oliver said. "Oh, hang on now… Jesus wept…"

Oliver studied a scene in Joe's mind, which quickly switched to Oliver being inside Joe as if he were him. He walked along a deserted street, staring around in every direction in order to make sure it was a safe place to be. He spotted a house ahead, more secluded than the others, and recognised it as the housing estate that had recently been boarded up ready to be demolished. Did Joe live there, was that it? Had he refused to move out of his home, be rehoused elsewhere?

Oliver approached that house, going inside and up the stairs to stand in a room he'd seen before.

"I know where he killed them," he whispered. "Not sure if I can get a definite location, but it's on that abandoned housing estate. In one of the houses. That's why there was grit and whatnot on the bodies. Dirt from beneath carpets. There's still some blood on the floorboards—he's angry with himself for not cleaning up properly, but I get the idea he didn't have time. He went back to get rid of it, but it had seeped into the wood, and he couldn't get it out."

Oliver was conscious of his voice carrying, of not being able to control its volume while he was so ensconced in Joe's body and mind, so stopped talking. He glanced out of a side window in the house. A beaten-up red Ford Fiesta was parked inside a cocoon of shrubbery—those women had been transported in it. Oliver still knew the number etched onto the light casing from Joe's original kill and recalled that when it had been run through the database, it had belonged to another car entirely. A Ford, but not a Fiesta.

A bell startled Oliver out of Joe's mind, and he riveted his attention on the door. Sylvia had entered and stood looking around. She didn't seem frightened, but when she spied him and Langham, she quickly averted her gaze elsewhere and visibly relaxed. She walked towards Joe's table and smiled down at him. He said something to her, and she sat, while he got up and went to the counter. Sylvia lifted one hand to her chest, and Oliver could only assume she was switching the hidden microphone on. Yes, there it was, her heavy breathing filtering into his earpiece, small buds he and Langham had each inserted out of sight prior to entering the café.

Oliver tensed. Her jagged breaths transferred to him as her being on the verge of mass panic, and who could blame the poor cow? No one thought they'd ever be a chosen victim. He hadn't, yet when he'd found out those twenty or so killers had intended to use him in the Queer Rites case like they'd used the other men they'd killed... Oliver had thought that was it for him. The end. That his life, for what it had been worth, would be snuffed out as easily as a damp finger and thumb pinching a lighted match.

Joe returned to the table, placing Sylvia's cup down carefully, setting a plate complete with doughnut beside it. She wouldn't feel like eating, but if she didn't, if she said she wasn't hungry, Joe, being as suspicious as he seemed to be at the moment, might become more so. The pastel-coloured sprinkles on top of the icing reminded Oliver of the Sugar Strands case, his first really big one where he'd been allowed to trail Langham throughout. Although this doughnut wouldn't be infused with drugs like the ones back then, he couldn't help but shudder as if it were. He wanted to get up, go over there, and take her away, keep her safe.

"Don't even think about it," Langham said. "She'll be fine. We're here. Villier's here."

"When will you arrest him?" Oliver wanted this over and done with. The tension was wreaking havoc with his stomach.

"Not sure. Playing it by ear."

"So," Joe said, his voice clear through the bud. "You came."

"I did," Sylvia said.

"How's the headache?" he asked.

She paused for a second or two, then seemed to remember she'd used that as an excuse as to why she couldn't meet him. "Oh, it's all right now. I took some tablets. They eased it a bit. I think I'm coming down with the flu or something. I don't feel right at all."

He frowned. "I sincerely hope not. I was really looking forward to you being an angel."

"I was, too, but if I'm ill, I'm ill, you know?"

"But you *can't* be ill," he said, reaching out to touch her hand.

What was it with this man? Didn't he even like her? Did he kill to rid the planet of women? What the hell was his agenda?

"Well," she said, "I can hardly help it if I am, can I?" She picked up the doughnut. "Thanks for this. You're so thoughtful."

"I try my best," he said. "So, have you given any more thought to knife play? Remember we talked about it in the club? I think you said you wouldn't mind if you didn't get hurt."

Oliver tensed at that.

"Oh, I don't know. I mean, we haven't even got to that stage yet, have we?" she said. "Haven't even reached first base, so to speak. Stuff like knives and being slapped or whatever comes later in a relationship, don't you think? Like, you have to be with someone for a while before you fully trust them. I'd be a bit of a moron if I let you use a knife the first time we got together like...that."

Joe nodded. "I see where you're coming from. I tend to forget that just because I know I'm a nice person and wouldn't hurt you, that you wouldn't know that."

"Slimy bastard," Oliver whispered.

"He's certainly got the patter down, hasn't he?" Langham said. "For all his worrying, the shit you and Sylvia sensed, he certainly seems calm now."

130

Sylvia took a bite of the doughnut, swallowed, then said, "No, I don't know anything about you really. We need to see each other more often, make sure we're compatible and all that."

"I'm glad you said that," Joe said. "I haven't been able to stop thinking about you since I saw you last. Kind of why I wanted to meet you now, before Friday. You know, spend a bit of time together."

"Lying motherfucker," Oliver mumbled.

"That's lovely," Sylvia said. "So are we staying here, or shall we go somewhere else? Chains, maybe?"

"No," he blurted, too quickly. "No, we won't go there. I thought maybe a drive would be nice. I have a second home. Thought maybe you'd like to see it?"

"Great!" Sylvia sipped some of her drink. "God, that's a bit hot. Burnt my tongue."

Joe's thoughts intruded. *More of you will get burnt soon, but not by fire. No, it'll be the heat of a blade. I know you're the one, the woman who will hit red on the wheel. It's tonight, you need to come with me tonight.*

Oliver leant across to Langham and whispered the information.

"Let's go," Joe said. "Right now."

He stood abruptly, his thigh bashing the table, the movement toppling his coffee cup. Sylvia stared up at him, her mouth hanging open, her eyes wide.

"What, *right* now?" she asked, barely keeping the panic from her voice.

"Yes."

He smiled at her, but it wasn't the kind of smile that would endear anyone to him. No, it was cold, merciless, and if they didn't stop this before it got too far, Sylvia might also experience the cold mercilessness of his knife.

CHAPTER SIXTEEN

In the car, Langham kept at what he hoped was a discreet distance. What with Joe changing his routine, the man might be jittery, might be on the lookout for someone following him. As they neared the deserted housing estate, Langham wondered how they were going to get around this obstacle. If he followed Joe onto it, there was no doubt he would cotton on to what was happening. But how could he let him go? The time taken for them to find where he'd gone on foot would be time wasted—time they didn't have. If Joe had escalated, he might kill her right away. Might not even go through his process of her spinning the wheel and dropping the ball bearing.

Sylvia chattered away to Joe, asking where his second home was.

"Oh, it's on the estate they're going to bulldoze. I moved out, got another place, but I can't help but still think of it as my real home. Lived there all my life," he said. "I think I'll go back until it's gone, razed to the ground, nothing but rubble."

"That's sad," she said. "Why are they knocking it down anyway?"

"Prefabs," he said. "Built quickly after the war. Most of them are basically on their last legs, a bit dangerous to live in. They've been empty for months, which makes me wonder why we all couldn't have stayed until the last minute. There hasn't been any indication of when they're actually going to get rid of them."

"Yeah, but if they're dangerous..." Sylvia didn't finish. Instead, she went on with, "So, is your furniture still in there?"

"Only a table and a post," he said.

"A post?" She sounded confused.

"Yes, you'll see what I mean when we get there."

"Do they still have the street signs up?" she asked.

134

"Yes. My place is on Gerald Drive, number sixty-two. I'll miss it when it's gone," he said. "There are so many memories wrapped up inside those bricks and cement."

"Aww," she said.

Langham grimaced. "I'll bet there fucking are." He took a left turn and sped along the streets, aiming to enter the estate from the other side, park up out of sight, then head for Gerald Drive. Lucky breaks didn't usually come so easily, and he intended to use this one for all it was worth.

"Clever of her to steer the conversation that way," Oliver said.

"It was." Langham nodded. "And now she'll have an idea she's kind of on her own, that we're not following. Probably why she's gone quiet. Well, apart from her heavy breathing."

"She'll be shitting herself." Oliver scrubbed at his chin.

Langham nodded again then contacted the station, relaying the address and asking for complete caution. The last thing he needed was uniforms swarming all over the place, alerting Joe to what was going on. Joe had hustled Sylvia out of the café too quickly for them to intervene, and she hadn't run off to get away from him. They'd had no choice but to tail the car to ensure her safety.

Villier responded, saying she was en route, and the two coppers who had been smoking outside the café then chipped in, saying much the same.

"Go around the back," Langham told them. "Stay in the garden if there is one, as close to the house

135

as you can, so if he looks out of the window he can't see you. If you get there before me, only make a move if you see him doing anything out of the ordinary."

Oliver said, "Tell them not to go down the side. He parks in the shrubbery there."

Langham passed the information on then trained his focus on what was ahead. He had it in mind to enter the house before Joe and Sylvia arrived, although how he'd do that without arousing Joe's suspicions he didn't know. Maybe the back door was his best bet. Going in through the front wasn't an option. He didn't have time to pick the damn lock so that their entry wasn't spotted. Kicking the door open would cause damage and give the game away.

He shook his head. "Fuck me, I seriously, *seriously* need a break from this kind of shit."

"Feeling a bit like that myself," Oliver said. "That holiday you were on about. Going to actually book time off like you said?"

"Yep. I'll get the paperwork done—for this case and the last—then fuck right off. We'll hole ourselves up in a hotel or whatever. Play cards. Get rat-arsed." He smiled.

Sylvia's breathing grew more ragged. "Oh, this is such a shame. Look at the empty houses. It's all so sad."

"It is, isn't it?" Joe said. "So you can probably understand why I find it difficult to stay away."

"Oh, I do. I really do…"

Oliver picked up on her thoughts.

136

Because this is where you bring women. And when your house is gone, you'll have nowhere else to take them that's as safe. Will I be the last one? Will you finish me off as well? Oh God. Please let those policemen stop this. I can't... I don't want to die. What if they don't get here in time? What if they have an accident or something? OhGodohGodohGod.

"She's panicking," Oliver said. "Really panicking. Thinks we won't get there."

"We're there already." Langham parked in Joblin Road, on a driveway beside a house that sat at the top of a cul-de-sac. "Through there"—he pointed ahead—"is Gerald Drive if my memory serves me right. If we go through and jump the fence, we'll be in one of the back gardens in Gerald. Then it's just a case of finding number sixty-two without being seen out the front."

"Right."

Oliver got out, and Langham followed, overtaking him as they entered the rear garden and legged it to the bottom fence. It was six-foot high, wooden slats that were rough and could give a nasty-arsed splinter or two. Langham vaulted it, getting his suit jacket caught, and after yanking it free—wincing at the sound of a rip—he dropped to the other side. Oliver fared better, getting over quickly, and they both ran towards the back of a house then scooted down the side.

Langham stared out into the street, sidling along the front of the house and quickly noting the door number. Eighty. So they were close. He peered across the road, conscious that at any moment Joe could pull into the street and spot them. He made out number sixty-one, sixty-three beside it. So they were numbered oddly, a damn stupid thing to do in his opinion. He'd never understood why developers had decided not to number the houses in order.

"Fuck it," he said, stepping over a pile of rubble, making his way across the garden. "We'll be seen at this rate." His heart hammered painfully, adrenaline leaking into his system, seeming to take the place of his blood. It streamed through his veins, leaving him momentarily weak.

"Down here." Oliver ran to the pavement outside number eighty. "It'll be on this side of the road."

Langham followed, relieved there were no cars—but that didn't mean Joe wasn't already here, his Fiesta parked in the shrubbery, him watching them from a window. Sixty-two was in the corner, and they moved down the side of that house, relief bleeding into Langham that the red car wasn't there, shrouded by leaves.

"Thank Christ for that," he breathed.

He made for the back, jumping a bit when he ran headlong into Villier.

"Shit, I thought it was him," she said, her face draining of colour.

"No, thankfully he isn't here yet." Langham went to the back door. Tried the handle. Locked. "Fuck's sake! You got a set of lock pickers on you?" he asked Villier.

138

"No, didn't have time. Didn't think. They're in my car."

"Shit, I did the same. Too busy concentrating on getting here." Langham cursed. "We'll just have to do it the old-fashioned way. Mind yourself." He stood still, cocking his head to listen. Didn't hear a car. "Right, it's now or never. Won't be long and he'll be here." He frowned. "Come to think of it, I haven't heard them speaking for a while."

"She's still breathing," Oliver said. "But it's steadier. Like she's sleeping."

"That bastard. I bet he's drugged her." Langham clenched his jaw then threw himself at the door, whacking his shoulder against the wood. It didn't budge, so he tried again. The door flung open, the momentum carrying Langham with it. He stumbled into a kitchen, managing to remain upright while staggering to the wall opposite. He came to a stop just before he crashed into it. "Upstairs." He looked at Oliver. "And you, Villier, stay down here. Close the door behind you. Try to get rid of the wood splinters as best you can in case he comes in here."

"There's nowhere for me to hide, sir," she said.

Langham glanced at her. "Then stay in the garden. Whatever. Just get yourself out of sight."

He moved through the kitchen then entered a hallway. The front door was opposite, two frosted glass panels in the top. Along with the hum of an engine, Langham caught a glimpse of the red vehicle as it went past.

"Quickly, upstairs." He made for them, checking over his shoulder that Oliver was behind him. "From what you saw"—he sucked in a breath, unfit and wishing he was the sort who went to a gym—"when Lisa and Tina showed you their time here, it sounded like a bedroom. You agree with that?"

"Yep," Oliver said. "I had a quick look in the living room. Wasn't the place."

"Right. Good."

At the top of the stairs, Langham rounded the newel post, thinking that ordinarily he would have arrested Joe after he'd parked, but Sylvia had gone with him willingly, and it was only a suspicion that she'd been drugged. They had to wait to see if that was the case before he could make a move.

All the doors were open apart from one. By instinct, Langham chose that one to go into. He opened the door, seeing he'd been right. A pale bloodstain marred the wooden flooring, and he was sickened to know that it had once travelled through the body of a vibrant young woman, now dead and awaiting burial. A pasting table had been set up, a box on top, the signpost Oliver had seen beside it.

"Christ..." Langham glanced around. "What's that there?"

He pointed to a door and, without needing a response from Oliver, went over to it. He pulled it open. A built-in wardrobe, empty of clothes.

"In here," he said, stepping inside and waiting for Oliver to join him.

140

It was a tight fit, the space narrow but high enough that they didn't need to crouch. Safe in the knowledge that Villier and perhaps the other two coppers were on guard downstairs, ready to step in if Joe decided to do Sylvia some damage as soon as he entered the house, Langham closed the door, thinking that leaving it ajar would be a bad move. If Joe had left it closed, he'd possibly remember, know that something was off if it was slightly open when he came in.

If he comes in…

The faint sound of a door opening filtered in. Langham's stomach rolled over, and he coached himself calm, not needing an extra blast of adrenaline to knock him off-kilter. He had to be on the ball, ready to pounce when the moment was right. The tread of footsteps on the stairs came next, and Joe murmuring something. His voice grew louder, as did the footsteps, and, judging by the even higher volume of him walking, he was in the room.

"So like I said, He will be pleased that I've brought you here earlier than planned." Joe's voice was different, held a note of extreme confidence. "I'm sure you'll be able to spin the wheel adequately enough. Even though you're a bit woozy and don't appear to be able to speak, we don't need words in order for you to perform your choice."

Langham was dying to see what was going on. He imagined Joe had carried her up here—there hadn't been two sets of footsteps—and the creak of the floorboards suggested he'd placed her down.

"That's it, you get comfortable there for a moment while I inspect the wheel. Then you can get up and stand beside me, make your choice, and I'll get to work."

Get to work? He sees this shit as a job?

Oliver shuddered beside him. God knew what he was seeing, but Langham wished that just for a few minutes he had the same abilities as him. To be able to see what was going on out there would be a big help in letting him know when the right time was to burst out and arrest that fucker's sorry arse.

"There," Joe said. "We're ready. Stand up now, please."

So polite...

There was a scuffle, and Langham imagined Sylvia struggling to her feet, her equilibrium shot to pieces. If she wanted to scream, to speak, it seemed the ability to do so had been stolen from her. What the fuck he'd injected the women with must be strong—Langham needed to ask Hank for the tox reports.

"Spin the wheel," Joe said. "Then drop the ball onto it."

The clatter of the ball being dropped then bouncing over the spinning wheel had Langham wanting to stop this insane madness right this second.

"Ah, the Lord is good. Red! We have red!" Joe shrieked.

Oliver nudged Langham sharply in his side, and Langham streaked out of the wardrobe. Joe spun around, knife in hand, and stared wide-eyed at Langham.

"You!" Joe said, grabbing Sylvia by her hair and yanking her to stand in front of him. "You're the men from the club."

Without answering, and quickly judging the situation, Langham lunged forward before Joe had the chance to do the one thing Langham didn't want him to—hold the knife at Sylvia's neck. He smacked into Joe's side, sending him and Sylvia sprawling away from him to land on their knees. Joe got up then spun again, knife out in front of him, and jabbed at the air with it, stopping Langham getting closer. In his peripheral, Oliver scooted around to Joe's other side. He hadn't been trained for this kind of thing, and any attempt he made at getting that knife from Joe would be an amateur's job.

Oliver struck out, chopping at Joe's wrist with the side of his hand. As the shock registered on the killer's face, Langham jolted, grabbing that wrist and wrestling the knife upwards. He squeezed, hard, and stared into Joe's eyes even harder, then twisted him so his back was to Langham's chest. Bringing Joe's wrist down repeatedly against his thigh, he waited until the knife dropped to the floor then jabbed him in the back of the knee so the man went down. On autopilot, he cuffed his wrists, read him his rights, and glanced sideways at Oliver.

Sylvia was cradled in his arms, the pair of them on the dirty floor, her eyes wide, her cheeks and lashes damp. Her mouth was open, a silent scream spewing out, and while Joe struggled against his hold, Langham knew he'd never forget the look on Sylvia's and Oliver's faces for as long as he lived.

Terror. It was a hideous thing to see.

CHAPTER SEVENTEEN

God had let him down. He should have known that would be the case. After all, hadn't he had to struggle through life, always fighting for what he wanted and never getting it? This job had been too good to be true, this journey worth nothing more than dog's muck on the underside of someone's shoe.

He smiled wryly and hunched farther into the corner on the narrow mattress on top of what was loosely termed a bed. It wasn't a bed, more like a wooden box painted white, the thin mattress not made for comfort. He supposed he'd get used to sleeping on it, but the luxury of a well-sprung resting place wasn't in his future. He hadn't convinced them he was mad, hadn't been transferred to the relative luxury of a mental asylum.

Once again, he hadn't got what he'd wanted.

He'd known he'd get caught eventually. As out of control as he'd become at the thought of God ignoring him, he should have realised meeting up with that Sylvia woman hadn't been his best move. But other voices had entered his head—those that didn't belong to God or any of his angels—and persuaded him that deviating from his usual method, earlier than he'd planned, had been the way to go. He acknowledged that his need for a slice killing had fuelled his desire to bring the murder closer, and that he should have waited for God's wise words before going ahead. Still, he'd tried, and his only concern now was that someone else would fare better than he had. That someone else would serve God in the way He should be served.

Closing his eyes, he listened to the sounds of other people in adjoining rooms. Some moaned, some just created a nasty racket. The tinny tune of some pop song or other came from a faraway radio. The pull of sleep tugged.

He sat bolt upright, his heart hammering, his smile wide.

God had spoken to him again. There were still jobs to do. Only he'd have to do them in here and be a bit wilier about it. And he would. After all, he could hardly be sent to prison again, could he?

He was already there.

Oliver propped his feet up on Langham's desk. He was knackered so hoped none of the dead wanted to speak to him once he got into bed later. Instead of leaving his mind open, he'd shut it off, closed the chink in the veil or whatever the hell it was so none of them could get through. If someone had died, they were still going to be dead in two weeks' time once he and Langham had had their lads' holiday.

Langham sighed, scribbling on his paperwork. "Enough is enough. I've given all I can for now. I'm exhausted, as are you."

"Yep."

Yet Langham still worked on.

Oliver was only hanging about as they were meant to be going to the pub. "You going to be much longer? There's a bloody pint with my name on it waiting for me."

Langham tossed his pen down. "Fuck it, let's go." He stood. "Before someone else sodding well carks it."

147

Printed in Great Britain
by Amazon

47611716R00088